A THOUSAND COUNTRY ROADS

~

an epilogue to

The Bridges of Madison County

ALSO BY ROBERT JAMES WALLER

Just Beyond the Firelight

One Good Road Is Enough

Iowa—Perspectives on Today and Tomorrow

The Bridges of Madison County

Slow Waltz in Cedar Bend

Old Songs in a New Café

Images

The Ballads of Madison County
(lyrics and music for Atlantic Records CD)

Border Music

Puerto Vallarta Squeeze

A
THOUSAND
COUNTRY
ROADS

~

an epilogue to

The Bridges
of Madison County

by

ROBERT JAMES WALLER

jmh

JOHN M. HARDY PUBLISHING
ALPINE & HOUSTON

2002

First printing: April 2002

5 7 9 10 8 6 4

A special, limited edition of 1500 copies,
numbered and signed by the author,
precedes this, the trade edition.

ISBN 0-9717667-1-1

Printed and bound in the United States of America

Book and dust jacket design – Leisha Israel
Blue Sky Media, Austin, Texas

John M. Hardy Publishing Company
Two Riverway, Suite 500
Houston, Texas 77056

www.johnmhardy.com

Once more,
for the peregrines,
the strangers,
last cowboys.

And for all the readers
who asked about
the rest of the story.

In all, a book of endings.

ACKNOWLEDGMENTS

Thanks to Mike and Jean Hardy of Iron Mountain Press and John M. Hardy Publishing for agreeing to publish the book and specifically to Jean for her diligent editing of the manuscript. Much praise must be given to Linda Bow, who not only read and commented on an early draft of the manuscript, but also generated the title, after at least fifty others had been considered and rejected. A number of my close friends read early versions of the book, and I am indebted to them, as well. Though I visited Big Sur several times as part of my research, Arlene Hess at the Carmel, California, library answered additional questions about that area, and the Big Sur Historical Society was helpful, as were the Henry Miller Library and the Astoria, Oregon, Chamber of Commerce. Photographer Linda Solomon's permission to use the photograph of Jack the Border collie and me on the dust jacket is greatly appreciated. Finally, thanks to my agent, Aaron Priest, for his advice and continued tolerance of my idiosyncratic ways.

AUTHOR'S NOTE

There are songs that come free from the blue-eyed grass, from the dust of a thousand country roads. This is one of them.

With those words I began a book called *The Bridges of Madison County*. But, in truth, there were two stories. Stories sometimes must wait their turn lest they clutter other things having first call. Over the years, letters arrived from the readers of *Bridges,* from men and women, teenagers of both genders, from truck drivers and housewives and lawyers and pilots and oil-rig workers. Hundreds of letters, probably thousands, from all over the world, with kind thoughts and good wishes.

A fair percentage of those who wrote wanted to know more about Robert Kincaid and Francesca Johnson, about their lives, about what happened to them after their four days together in Madison County, Iowa. Living a quiet, contented existence on a remote, high-desert ranch, having returned to my studies of economics and mathematics and jazz guitar, I felt no need to dig out the research notes, no push to write more. Yet, somewhere, at some time, for reasons not clear, after reading one more letter requesting information, I decided to tell the rest of the story.

And I wonder always about improbabilities, the nature of chance. *The Bridges of Madison County,* a small story set in a small time, a book originally written as a gift for family and friends, a book I never had any hope of getting published nor intentions of doing so when I wrote it, in thirty-five or more languages now. A book that rolled from an inexpensive printer when I was using five-dollar software on a chugging Zenith 286 computer.

So, for those of you who asked and for anyone else with such curiosity, here is the rest of the story. If you have not read *Bridges,* the book may not stand by itself for you. For those who have read *Bridges,* I think you will find, among other things, surprise at the unexpected joy Robert Kincaid discovered late in his life.

ROBERT JAMES WALLER
In the Texas high-desert
Del Norte Mountains
New Year's Eve, 2001

Robert Kincaid

So:

> Come twirl the big rope again,
>   maybe not so high and wild
>   as you once did,
>   but still
>   with the hiss
>   and feel
>   of the circle
>   above you
>   and sun falling through the loop,
>   shadows on the ground
>   where the big rope twirls
>   while it's all getting down
>   to last things,
>   down to one-more-times...

...down to inevitabilities and the long winding run from where you rocked in your mother's darkness to this: fog over Puget Sound and sitting in Shorty's bar on Tuesday nights, listening to Nighthawk's tenor saxophone contemplate "Autumn Leaves."

So this as it stands, the end of your season on the line and still alone, with the refrigerator's hum laid over the sound of your memories. Last cowboys and all that. Those who hammered out the trace for you going or gone, Iris packing up her rainbow and the scholars of the twilight dead. Now, only the sound of your memories and the refrigerator's hum and Nighthawk's tenor on Tuesday nights.

It might have been different in a different life. Might have worked out for you and the woman. She was your one chance, and yet looking back on what happened, there was no chance at all. You have always known that, probably knew it then.

The act of going, of leaving what she had, that in itself would have made her a person apart from the one with whom you spent those days and nights. Both the decision and the act would have done that. Still, you would have risked it and tried to work things out on the run if she had turned your way.

Now, early morning in November 1981, chilly fog over the water. And piles of mail on the kitchen table you picked up for five dollars at a yard sale. Lugged it here on a ferry years ago after they bulldozed the apartment house in Bellingham to build a shopping center. Envelopes with a veneer of officialdom—government stuff—the VA and Social Security people still trying to find you. They can't figure out you might not want to hear from them, that you don't want whatever they're offering. Those envelopes marked: Return to Sender.

Still, it's mail of some kind when there's little else in the box except advertisements from people trying to get you to buy things you don't care about owning, home theater systems and such. Thinking, what the hell is a home theater system, anyway?

And if you had the money to buy it, which you don't, what would you do with it?

At the age of sixty-eight, Robert Kincaid tugged on a frayed orange suspender and ran his other hand along the neck of a golden retriever called Highway. He lit a Camel and walked to the window. Somewhere in the fog or behind the fog, low distant ronnk of a tug working the Seattle harbor.

Kincaid opened the top drawer of a four-high filing cabinet near the window. The rows of photographic slides hanging in their plastic pages, his life in those pages, five to a row and twenty to a page. The life of a man who had spent his years looking for good light. He chose a page at random and held it up to a reading lamp. The first slide was of a dock worker in Mombasa, muscles popping and big grin under a knit cap. That would have been 1954, twenty-seven years earlier.

The second was of a harp seal pup looking straight up the lens at him: 1971 and the ice floes off Newfoundland. Then along the Strait of Malacca and men putting out to sea in a six-oar boat, fishing with baited hooks and dwindling hope waters fished too long and hard. After that, a summer shot in the Basque countryside. And a cold June along the Beaufort Sea where Amundsen had once sailed. And a tiger coming out of long grass on the shores of Lake Periyar in south India. Another pocket showed a heron looping across morning water near Port Townsend, the photo looking much like the sound of Nighthawk's saxophone on the fourth measure of "Sophisticated Lady."

More. The *campesino* girl in Mexico, standing
in a field and looking back over her shoulder at
him, floppy straw hat and feed-sack dress, her
name and village neatly lettered along one edge of
the slide: *María de la Luz Santos, Celaya, Mexico,
1979.* That had been his last major assignment for
a magazine, a low-budget shoot where he eventually used some of his own money to get the job
done right. He wondered whatever happened to
María de la Luz Santos, if she still lived in the
same village and worked the fields of summer.

Next pocket, the sun slowly falling through a
North Dakota autumn and a hard, sunglassed face
looking down from the window of a big orange
machine: *Jack Carmine, Wheat Combiner, farmer's
field south of Grand Forks, 1975.*

Thousands of photographs in the file. Robert
Kincaid had kept only the best ones, and his stan-
dards were exquisitely high. The rejects tossed and
burned as part of the sorting. For each of those he
kept, he could remember almost the exact time
and place and light conditions when he hit the
shutter. Even the smells that had surrounded him.
Periyar brought him curry, the Basque shot
returned spiced goat meat. The Beaufort shoot
had been a less interesting culinary experience, the
tedium of camp food mainly, fish sometimes, all of
it forked in under mosquito netting.

The last slide in the page was a blurred image of
rock and water. He was working the cliffs of Acadia
in 1972 and had slipped and fallen thirty feet to
sand just as he pressed the shutter. He kept the
shot as a token to daring and stupidity and the thin

edge separating them. The broken ankle had never healed properly, chiefly because he ignored his physician's advice and started working hard before the bone had a proper chance to mend. He returned the page to its place and rested easy on the open drawer, hands folded on the files, fingers laced.

At the front of the drawer was a large manila envelope containing letters written to Francesca Johnson over the years, but never mailed. Behind the envelope was an archival box with photographic prints in it. Robert Kincaid took out the box and cleared a space on the kitchen table, pushing aside dirty dishes and advertisements and return-to-sendered VA letters. Lowering himself onto a chair and carefully opening the box, he put on his wire-rimmed bifocals and lifted a sheet of protective paper. He stared at the woman in the top photograph.

From sixteen years back, Francesca Johnson leaned on a fence post in Iowa and smiled at him in her old jeans and T-shirt. Black and white had been right for her, picked up the lines of her body and the lines in her face, just the way she looked back then. When he first printed the shot, she came up on the paper like the ghost of his past she was. First the blank paper, then the soft outlines of meadow and fence and a human form, then Francesca in high contrast at dawn on a Wednesday, in August, in 1965. Francesca, coming toward him out of the tray.

Robert Kincaid studied the photograph, as he had hundreds of times over the years since being there with her. There were twenty-six other shots of her in the box, but this was his favorite. Nothing fancy, just Francesca and the morning, her breasts pressing against thin cotton and clearly outlined against it.

He laid his hands on the table beside the box, spread his long, slim fingers, and felt the touch of her skin from back through all the years. Felt the shape of her body, some tactile memory from his mind to his hands or the other way around. Without moving his hands, only his mind, he could run them easy and soft over her, the length and round of her, over Francesca Johnson.

Francesca and his one chance at wrenching aside all the lonely times, his one damn chance at something other than these long years of silence and solitude, the road and the roar of jet engines on his way to wherever the light was good. He would have given up everything for her, the road and the picture-making, anything. But there were choices in the way of them, hard choices for her. And she had made her decision, the right one as she saw things, and stayed with it. Stayed with her family in Iowa instead of leaving with him.

Jesus, how he could bring it back, convert images into feelings, make it torturously real and right there for him. His belly against hers, the arch of her body as she came to him, the lightning of a thick summer night though the bedroom curtains. Her soft smile and how she couldn't stop touching him, there in the bed, the morning after, always with her hands on him.

"If I don't touch you, I'm afraid this all might go

away," she told him, smiling and pressing against him as she said it.

But it went away just the same. Went away on a Friday morning when he drove down the lane of her farm in southern Iowa, when the sun was hot and the trees were still and the world had a silent heart. When he stood on the running board of a truck named Harry and looked back up the lane at her, looked a long time before taking Harry slowly onto the main road. And tears coming then as he glanced back one time at Francesca sitting where the lane began, sitting cross-legged with her head in her hands, in the heat and dust of an Iowa summer.

Who the hell says the fires burn down? Maybe flicker a little, but never snuffed completely. The old myths, a matter of convenience for those who no longer want the press of a woman against them and all the responsibilities that entails. Looking at the photo of Francesca Johnson, his hands moving over her across the miles and years, he wanted it all again, wanted her naked and moving beneath him and saying words he could not always understand, but understood just the same. He felt himself starting to get hard, and smiled. Just the thought of her could still do that to him.

Robert Kincaid removed his billfold from the left hip pocket of his jeans and extracted a small piece of folded paper. The paper was smudged and raggedy from a thousand unfoldings and ten thousand readings of Francesca Johnson's words with a phrase from W.B. Yeats embedded in them.

If you'd like supper again when 'white moths are on the wing,' come by tonight after you're finished. Anytime is fine.

Her handwriting from a long-ago summer when August had been hot and stayed that way and he sipped iced tea in her plain farmhouse kitchen. Later that night, she tacked the invitation to the side of a covered bridge, Roseman Bridge, in Madison County, Iowa.

Just to talk with her, to say again how he felt, how his entire life had been made whole for a few days. To thank her, if nothing else, look at her, see her face again. One moment of being able to say he was still out there and still loved her. Not possible and never was possible, her with a family and all. He leaned back, ran his hands through his gray hair, which was disheveled as usual, hanging two inches beyond his shirt collar. Final things, one-more-times, and the road still out there. Last cowboys ought to twirl the big rope again. Ought to do that. Ride the tired horse until it falls and let the blunted stem of your evolutionary path end with your passing.

Crouched there with fog on the water, fog at the door, and the footprints of all the years upon him. Crouched at the edge of...what? Nothing.

He poured a cup of coffee, walked to the cupboard, and opened it. On the shelves lay his equipment: the five lenses capped and resting in soft leather bags, the two Nikon F's and the Rangefinder, wrapped in thick cloth. The tools of a professional, old tools, old and battered, scratched and scarred from metal buttons and zippers, from sirocco-driven sand and rocks of the Irish Barrens, from the jostling and rubbing of miles in Harry and in transcontinental jets bound for Africa or Asia or somewhere.

In the freezer compartment of the refrigerator was his last roll of Kodachrome II 25-speed film. When they stopped making it, he bought five hundred rolls and kept them frozen, rationing and nursing them, holding them for his own use while the magazines shifted over to Kodachrome 64.

So it all came down to this, just as he always knew it would. Fog on the water, fog at the door, and his last roll of film. The basics: blood and bone and flesh on the bones and thoughts in the mind, all gone to ashes come the end of things. Nothing more and impossible to change, the great push of what was written firm early on and stored by the Keepers of the way things turn out. What a strange, lonely, silent life. From the beginning it was of that feather and stayed the same. Except for those days, those four lambent days in 1965.

Down to this, after the years of walking Acadia's cliffs and the shores of Africa's horn, after twilights in a mountain village where the universe slides together, the laughing swims in jungle pools with a silk-merchant's daughter, her laughter pushing the silence away only for a moment. And always, always, being aware of the howl of time, of the fading and passing of this curious thing known as life, of understanding it was all so transitory. Work, eat, walk straight and stagger later on. Watching it all come down to a four-high file of emulsions as fleeting as you are. Only the images remain, hushed testimony to your earlier celebrations.

> *India,*
> *or the Horn of Africa,*
> *or the Strait of Malacca,*
> *always the same:*
> *men on the sand,*
> *or handling boats*
> *in the shore waves.*
> *Some go*
> *while others watch.*
> *Tomorrow*
> *they will do it*
> *...again.*

~

Once the idea came to him, it wouldn't leave. He walked to the window and looked at the fog. Even the morning seemed tired, though it had only begun.

Robert Kincaid opened a kitchen drawer. Three uncashed checks from wearisome shoots at schools and art fairs, totaling $742. Not the glory days anymore, not the long wandering shoots for *National Geographic* that had taken him to wherever the light was good.

Another eighty-seven dollars in bills. His coffee can full of change had maybe fifty more in it. The new engine in Harry was carrying only sixty-eight thousand miles. Stay low, travel light, sleep in the truck, if necessary. He could do it, he could go there one more time, he and Highway.

"Well, Highway, think we ought to do it? Just go there, see Roseman Bridge, remember a lot of old things? Nothing else, just go stand in her space again. Better than sitting around here feeling sorry for myself, watching what the autumn does to leaves and butterflies, crying up for what's never going to be."

Highway, panting lightly and wagging his tail, came over to sit beside Robert Kincaid.

"I wonder what she looks like now. Wonder if she's changed much?"

Pine trees outside, mantled in haze, dripping. Flop of the dog's tail on the pine floor. Flop again.

Live alone for most of sixty-eight years, by choice and by circumstance, and your thoughts curl back upon themselves because there is no one else to hear them or make sense of them if they did hear. Eventually, though, they stream in random fashion from mind to tongue. As if your brainworks can no longer be contained in silence, and words must get outside so other thoughts can take their place.

A day or two, hours perhaps, of being absolutely alone and moving through continual silence are enough to start the process for most people. Robert Kincaid had lived a lifetime that way. He talked to himself while organizing a photograph he wanted to make, or while cooking his meals, mumbling about shutter speeds or spices, cameras or cheese. The dog had become a happy recipient of Kincaid's outward thoughts and, significance be damned, was content with only the sound of words directed toward or past him.

"Her kids'd be grown, gone probably. Couldn't take a chance on seeing her, anyway. Wouldn't know for sure what to do if I did see her. Don't know what she'd do, either. Hell, maybe it was just those four days and she's forgotten the whole thing. Just some memory that maybe she doesn't even like to think about anymore."

Robert Kincaid knew better. Francesca Johnson and he were locked into one another for as long as their minds would remember. He never really doubted that. Down all the roads he had gone in these last sixteen years, she was there. He knew, he was certain, it had to be the same for her. But sometimes the hurt lessened if he imagined she no longer thought about him, made it easier to endure the spear in his chest when he did think of her.

One great love in one dancing moment when the wind had come around to his back and the universe hesitated in whatever the universe was up to. One dancing moment when the old traveler saw the fires of home, when the trains came to rest and their whistles turned silent. When his circling around Rilke's ancient tower had ceased for a time.

Behind him the refrigerator grumbled into life, and Robert Kincaid smoked another Camel, coughed twice, and looked at the morning before him. He remembered the old farmhouse kitchen in Iowa. Like the ultimate and almost unerring witness he had been to life in general, the natural and practiced photographer's eye as a camera all its own, he could see it yet, the kitchen, the details.

The cracked linoleum and Formica table, the radio by the sink and moths around the light.

And Francesca there, looking at him, in her pink dress and white sandals. Francesca Johnson, taking the biggest chance of her life and falling toward him, he toward her. If sin exists, theirs was a mutual one, evenly divided and shared as equals. He stood there on that evening, leaning against her refrigerator, looking at her, at where the dress hem rested on the thigh of her slim brown leg. And then the insistent push of the old ways—let us at once praise and curse them—the old ways winning and the street tangos sounding far off but getting closer.

The old ways, wound in the tangled bed sheets of a hot summer night and skating on the sweat of Francesca's belly and her face and breasts, and sweat on his shoulders and face, and on his back and belly, too. The old ways and their sweet veronicas, the sweep of the crimson fighting cape and the roar of distant crowds unable to see the event but applauding anyway. All her years of suppressed wanting, all his years of the same, the two of them coming at each other over and over while the candles dripped and the rains came and left, and a tentative dawn rolled over the south Iowa countryside.

At first light, he had taken her into the pasture and asked her to lean against a fence post. And there he changed her into an image of black and white, which now lay in a box on a table, in another kitchen, on a foggy morning in Seattle.

Twirl the big rope again. Harry was wet and smelled of tobacco smoke. The same routine, intentionally the same routine as sixteen years before.

Suitcase wedged against the spare tire in the truck box and tied down with a length of clothesline rope. No guitar this time; he hadn't played for years. Thought about it, went back into the cabin and dug the guitar out of its space next to the refrigerator. The case was mildewed and hard to say what the guitar looked like, so he didn't bother to open the case. He shrugged and carried it out to the truck, tying it down beside the suitcase and pulling a piece of tarpaulin over both the guitar and suitcase. The guitar had given off a soft amusical sound from inside its case when he yanked the rope tight, as if it might be coaxed to play again if it were taken from darkness and tuned and touched.

At one time, Robert Kincaid would have jumped down from the truck box, but now he sat on the tailgate and gently slid off, putting first his good leg to the ground, then the one that would fail him if he weren't careful.

One camera knapsack only, with one Nikon F and a single lens—his favorite 105-millimeter—and his only roll of Kodachrome II. Just that one roll of film for an expedition called Last Time.

Thermos, camera, suitcase, three cartons of Camels, a case of Chinese beer he had found on sale at a waterfront store. Old sleeping bag. If money ran short, it might come down to camping in the truck. The tattered copy of *The Green Hills of Africa*, the book he took with him in 1965 and had not read since. He looked down at himself: the Red Wing field boots with their fourth pair of soles, faded jeans, khaki shirt, and his orange suspenders. Tan mountain parka behind the seat, with one ripped pocket and a coffee stain on the right sleeve. The unchanging, functional uniform of a swagman.

Highway on the seat beside him. Highway's jug of water and tin dish on the passenger-side floor next to a sack of dog food and the coffee can full of change.

An alternate route, though. Stay out of the night cold that would be settling in the far north country this time of year. In fact, no particular route at all, since there was no point in plans anymore. South to Oregon for a start, California after that, then east. Iowa wasn't moving anywhere, last he heard, and a general easterly direction from northern California would do it.

Maybe wander up through South Dakota and visit the Black Hills again, as he did on his last trip to Madison County, Iowa. He returned to the Hills in 1973 and photographed a story on an archeological dig, one of his last pieces for a major publication. The cantankerous old man who had served as his guide might still be around. Maybe stop and say hello, go over to whatever that tavern was called and listen to the accordion player if he was still there. Robert Kincaid sat straight in the truck seat and stared through the windshield, letting the feel of all that was out there and all that he had never seen come into him.

"You know, dog, I'm getting a little tired, myself, of all this gloom and doom I've been wallowing in. Maybe you are, too. Canting about the old ways and old days, shuffling around here looking at files of the things I used to be and do. Cursing the barbarism of senescence, giving up and turning my life into a real piece of ugly pie. Not like me. Reality is one thing, but a whittling down of dreams is next door to dying slow."

He paused for a moment, looked over at the dog. "Ever hear those wonderful lines by that other Cummings? Not our friend Nighthawk, but Mr. e. e. cummings, who liked to spell his name with small letters. Let's see...well, I can't remember all of it...something about doctors and hopeless cases and better universes somewhere else if you just go look for them."

He smiled at the dog. "Be back in a minute."

In the cabin Robert Kincaid took a knapsack from its place on the closet shelf and grabbed a scarred Gitzo tripod leaning against the back closet wall, behind the four shirts hanging there. Scrounging around on the closet floor, he found a black wool turtleneck sweater he had bought in Ireland years ago and draped the sweater over the Gitzo. His photographer's vest swung from a hanger. He took it down and slipped into it.

From the kitchen cupboard, he loaded cameras and accessories into the knapsack, neatly packing each in its place. He still had forty-three rolls of Tri-X black-and-white film in a drawer, the rolls scattered over the face of a plaque from a prestigious photography magazine:

TO ROBERT L. KINCAID
IN RECOGNITION
OF A LIFETIME OF EXCELLENCE
IN THE PHOTOGRAPHIC ARTS
Animus non integritatem sed facinus cupit
The heart wills not purity but adventure

He scooped the film into a plastic grocery bag, looked around, slung the tripod and sweater over one shoulder and the knapsack over the other. Locking the cabin, he was careful not to let the screen door slam as he closed it.

Back in the truck. "Ready, dog?" he asked and started the engine. "Let's go see what we might have missed along the way."

A thin sun sparred with midmorning fog while Robert Kincaid rode the ferry to the mainland, across the Sound and into Elliot Bay. Easy chop on the water. He took back streets out of town, working along the harbor, past the park where he and Nighthawk sometimes sat on a bench and told each other what they believed to be the truth about their lives. In Olympia, he cashed the school checks and dropped a postcard to Nighthawk, saying he was going out of town and would see him in a couple of weeks. Old men worry about each other, and his friend Nighthawk might wonder and worry.

He decided to take the coast roads south and swung west near Maytown, into open country, his kind of country, back roads and small towns. Highway, with his head out the window and ears flapping in the wind.

So it came, in November of 1981 and getting down to last things and one-more-times, trapped in the corners of the wire, Robert Kincaid twirled the big rope again and headed toward Iowa, to the bridges of Madison County.

2

Francesca

Francesca Johnson didn't feel old and didn't look the sixty years she carried. Her friends said that to her often, how time had been uncommonly good to her. How her black hair had never grayed beyond the few streaks appearing in her forties, how her figure retained its proportions.

Richard had remarked on that, too. "Frannie, while the rest of us are just getting older, I think you're never gonna change much."

But, of course, she had changed. Looking in her bureau mirror, she knew her clothes covered well the long slide down. Still, a good diet and a good outlook, wide-brimmed hats and her daily walk, a walk sometimes taking her the four miles to Roseman Bridge and back, kept her well together. More than that, there was always the thought that she might see him again, that in some way Robert Kincaid might come back to her. And perhaps more than anything, that sustained her will to stay as good and true as possible to the way she had looked years before. She wanted him to recognize her, wanted him to want her as much as he had wanted her all those years ago.

Her instrument of measure was a light pink dress she purchased in 1965. During the last sixteen years, she occasionally tried it on. If it seemed a little snug, she worked harder on her weight until the dress wore light and easy upon her. Wearing it, she slowly would turn before the mirror in her bedroom and smile and say to her own reflection, "It's about as good as I can do, but it's pretty good for a country girl." Then she would puff her cheeks and softly laugh at her self-congratulatory words. And the folded dress again would be wrapped in plastic and placed far up on a closet shelf.

Richard had died the year before, and the farm was not the same. Livestock sold, land rented out. Children grown and gone to where children go when the time comes. Not much money, but enough to get by with land rent and savings and Richard's small life insurance policy.

And now Richard lay in the Winterset cemetery, beside his parents. The solemn rows getting longer with parents and children in a line, notches in the earth to mark the passing of things. Richard had bought two gravesites in the cemetery, assuming Francesca would rest there beside him. He was wrong in that assumption, as later events would show.

Richard. Good, kind Richard. Decent without question and even loving in his own clumsy fashion. But it had not been enough for her. The Francesca that Richard had known was only camouflage, the surface of another woman lying beneath the dutiful farm wife and caring mother. Such layers, such lies of a kind. A whole other woman than the one who fried eggs and poked at bacon in the morning while Richard caught the early market reports on the kitchen radio. The same radio that had played "Tangerine" and "Autumn

Leaves" on a hot August night in 1965, while she danced in the kitchen with the man named Robert Kincaid who had blown into her life on a summer wind with a purpose all its own.

Standing there at the stove, she would think, my god, if he knew. If Richard only knew what had gone on in her kitchen. Could he imagine her there, naked and making love with a long-haired photographer from some other place than time present? Paper napkins drifting across the kitchen and onto the floor as Robert Kincaid laid her on the table? No. Richard never would have even thought it. Such lies and lies, such layers of a kind.

Still, Richard had a sense of it all. His deathbed words, a muted, scratchy sound deep in his throat only a few hours before he became unconscious. "Francesca, I know you had your own dreams, too. I'm sorry I couldn't give them to you."

With effort, then, with most of what remained of his strength, Richard moved his hand slowly across the hospital bed when he said those words, and she saw in his eyes gone wet and old that he was trying to say even more than what was contained in his words. She took his big, rough hand and laid her cheek on it, sorry in those moments, just in those few moments, for what she had done with Robert Kincaid. And equally sorry Richard would never know what lay so far inside her that she had been almost unaware of it herself, until the man named Kincaid rolled through her life.

Still, for all that he was not and never could be, Richard Johnson had known something more than she ever thought he knew. He knew something that hurt him hard and deep, that he was not of Francesca's dreams, that he had been married to her for over thirty years and still could never reach beyond the exterior woman who shared his working life and gave him children.

The old house was silent. Francesca unfolded the current edition of *The Madisonian* and read about the comings and goings of country people. Turning the pages chronicling church suppers and end-of-the-season football games, marriages and births and deaths, the events of a world in which she had lived for thirty-six years and of which she still did not feel a part.

Six months after Marge Clark died, Floyd had asked her out for dinner. She made tactful excuses and said no. He asked again when the county fair came around, something about calf judging and a barbecue. She tried to be gentle with him, making more excuses about being busy and children visiting. Floyd Clark did not ask again. But he was polite when their grocery carts met at the Fareway store. Floyd was thinning a bit and looked as if he missed Marge's cooking.

She laid the paper down and took off her glasses, staring far across the stubbled fields of autumn, letting Robert Kincaid come into her mind. He was always there, though for certain passing moments on certain passing days, it seemed as if he were nothing more than a fantasy she had run through her mind so many times it had become real. But there were the photographs of her he had sent, and the pictures of him and by him in *National Geographic*.

She wondered if he still was on the road, or if he was anywhere at all. Sometimes she stared at the contrails of a jet airplane far above and imagined Kincaid was up there, heading for Jakarta or Nairobi. Maybe she could have traveled to the Northwest and looked for him. Or maybe it was better just to live on what she remembered of him. Perhaps just those four days they had shared were all they were meant to have.

She might have found him, and after a few questioning looks and jogging his memory ("Oh yes, the woman from Iowa in the time of covered bridges"), he would have been his well-mannered, quiet self. They might have had coffee in a restaurant and talked for a few minutes before he would have looked at his watch and excused himself, saying he needed to do this or that.

And she would have been left sitting there in a red vinyl booth by herself, a long way from home, wishing she had never gone to find him. And living thereafter with the sadness that she was nothing more than a pleasant and fleeting interval in the life of a road man. Living thereafter with the destruction of all that had sustained her over the years. Living thereafter in the silence of a formless life.

No. That was not true. She was sure of it, most of the time. But it had been years ago, and if not for the pictures in *National Geographic,* she knew his face would be blurred in what she could remember of it. Yet those were old pictures, and she might not even recognize him. He would be sixty-eight. The leopard at sixty-eight, that was hard to imagine. He might be sick or otherwise diminished and wouldn't want her to see him that way.

Francesca went upstairs to her bedroom and took the pink dress from the closet shelf where it lay. In the corner of the room was the record player Carolyn had left behind. Wearing the pink dress, she put the phonograph needle down, listened to "Autumn Leaves" again, and looked at herself in the mirror, smiling and remembering the man named Robert Kincaid who had loved her more than she could ever have imagined being loved.

It was time for her walk. She changed into jeans and a denim shirt and went downstairs, glanced at the calendar and remembered her birthday was approaching.

And while she had been turning before her mirror, Robert Kincaid was coming up on the Pacific Ocean, running easy in the old truck named Harry, watching the countryside and talking to a dog named Highway. As he approached the water and turned south, Robert Kincaid, writer-photographer, or so he had called himself at one time, flexed his bad ankle and wished again, and in ways beyond counting, for all the things that never were.

3

Carlisle McMillan

Through the curves and switchbacks of a somewhat divergent life, Carlisle McMillan had come to
live in Yerkes County, in western South Dakota.
The circuitous way in which he came to that deso-
late place and the remarkable events that would
eventually encompass him—what came to be
known as the Yerkes County War—is yet another
story for another time.

For now, it is enough to say that Carlisle
McMillan was a master carpenter who had learned
his trade from an old man in northern California.
Worn of city life, depressed by the downward slide
of both his skills and his self respect from working on thrown-together housing developments,
Carlisle had taken his savings and launched himself
on a long, desultory run through America. In
Yerkes County, he found what he was looking for,
a place as far removed as possible from the onrush
of a world he didn't understand or, as time went
on, didn't care very much about understanding.
The first year of his life in South Dakota was spent
rebuilding an old house resting on thirty acres,
roughly eight-and-a-half miles north of a town that
will be called Salamander here.

As with most lives, his had been shaped through
chance as much as intent, by incident as much as
cunning. A decision here, another one there. Some

of them good in retrospect, others bad. The outcomes of his choices having been determined by rational effort mixed with unforeseen events arching in over his shoulder on days when he least expected them. The roll and toss of ordinary existence, in other words. Uncertainty, in another word.

And from the start, he had lived with more uncertainty than most. Thirty-five years back he had been born the misbegotten son of a woman named Wynn McMillan and a man whose last name she either never knew or could not remember. From what little his mother recalled and told him, he possessed no more than a vague and shifting image of the man who was his father.

So in his boyhood wonderings, and even the same in his later years, he saw the man only as a dark, knife-edged silhouette on a road bike, one of the big ones designed for long hauls. The silhouette rode the coastal highway south of Carmel, backlit by a falling sun, crossing a high bridge where the Pacific gouged deep into the cliffs. And the woman behind the rider? Her arms around his waist, her hair riffling back in the wind? That would have been the mother of Carlisle McMillan, a long time ago.

She and the man were together only a few days, but a few days were enough. Enough to create a boy-child named Carlisle.

She remembers the sand was warm against her back where she lay with him. She has never forgotten that, how warm was the sand in late September. And she remembers his strange, subdued ways. Haunted ways, almost, some of the same characteristics she later recognized in her son. She said he had

been gull-like in his movements, that he knew secret
things and heard faint music from a distant past that
was his alone. Yet, his last name escaped her. She
thinks he told her once, but they were sitting by an
evening fire, high on the rim of their lives, drinking
homemade beer. And she doesn't remember it.

As she once said, "Names seemed unimportant in
those days. I know it must be hard for you to understand, Carlisle, but that's how we felt. I suffer that,
more for you than for me."

So ran the edge of the tale. She told it to him
when he was twelve, while they sat on the front
steps of their rented house in Mendocino. She put
her arms around the thin, reserved boy and leaned
her head against his while she talked, freshly washed
hair conspicuous in her blend of mother scents. He
listened and loved her for the unrelenting honesty
with which she spoke, for the happiness she found
in having brought him to be, even for the tingling
overtones of mystical, sexual abandon she conveyed
in talking about the man. Though at Carlisle's age it
was hard for him to imagine anything of that sort,
especially involving his mother.

All of this was good, her honesty and her caring,
but it was not enough. In his secret places Carlisle
McMillan wished for a father then, a male who
could give reassurance that all the random and powerful feelings thrashing around inside him could
eventually be synthesized into a coherent, useful
manhood.

And for a long time he was angry. Angry about
the ambiguity, about Wynn McMillan casually mat-
ing with a formless creature who then rode north

through the coloring trees of a long-since autumn and simply disappeared. It took some living, some thinking, but he finally made a slender peace with it all. Well, most of it.

His mother and the man had come together in the fall of 1945, when World War II had just ended. Things were in a tipsy state of disarray, flowing from the sweet fume of victory coupled with lives put off and passions held in abeyance. If all of that were mixed with the happy improvidence of the Big Sur bohemian life, the poets and artists, including Henry Miller newly in from Paris and slouching along the road from Partington Ridge and peddling his watercolors, it became understandable. By the time he was thirty, Carlisle decided he probably would have done the same thing.

Still there was the ambiguity, the sense of being incomplete, and the curiosity about the particular ripple in the gene pool from which he came. There were those who said he looked part Indian, the cheekbones and the prominent nose, and the long brown hair he sometimes tied with a red bandana, Apache style. He kind of liked that idea, even though he had no way of knowing the truth or falsity of it. When people asked, "Do you have Indian blood?" he was silent, shrugging his shoulders, letting them draw their own conclusions.

And there was the tapping. That's what he called it. It had started early on and stayed with him over the years. Something way back and far down, source unknown. Blinking signals, faint and distant, maybe from the spirals of his DNA, coming when there was a stillness inside of him, feeling the signals more than hearing them. As if something furred were playing with a dusty telegraph key in a ghost-town railway station: tap... pause... tap... pause... tap, tap... repeat sequence.

Such was one pattern; there were others.

It seemed implausible to him at first, chimerical perhaps, but he imagined his father was sending a throttled message down the bloodlines to him. He thought of it this way: *My father as a person does not know I exist, but his genetic codes know, for they are part of me. The codes know I exist, the species knows I exist. I am of his species and carry his genetic blueprints. Therefore, in a way, he knows.* The logic was a little fuzzy, but it made sense if he didn't press it too far.

So Carlisle came to believe his father was back there someplace and listened when the signals began. He listened hard and talked back to them. "Who are you, man? Dammit, crank up the volume, stay on the air. Tell me something about you so I can know more about me. What is it I know that I don't know I know?" But the signals were tenuous, fading almost as soon as they started, and he always felt slightly abandoned and a little sorry for himself after that.

In place of a father who was but never was, and a subsequent stepfather with whom he never made a connection, Carlisle found an elderly carpenter named Cody Marx who became his surrogate father. And from Cody Marx had come Carlisle McMillan's skills as a carpenter and an outlook, the drive to do things right. Work to close tolerances in all things, Cody used to say.

A year after settling in Yerkes County, his house mostly finished, Carlisle sat at a small trestle desk he had built from scrap lumber and wrote his mother.

October 14

Hi Wynn,
I hope you're well. Any new cello students? Still working at the art gallery? The house has turned out pretty nice, thanks as always to Cody's training, and I've been picking up a little outside work. In fact, quite a lot of outside work. There are old buildings around here with well-cured lumber in their beams and siding, and most of the farmers, who seem to prefer metal buildings, are happy to let me have them just for the demolition and hauling off the good stuff along with the junk. Coming by lots of fine, aged woods that way.
Though I've threatened to do it for years, maybe it's time to look for some thread of my father. I know it has been a lot of years, but try once again, think hard. Anything you can remember will help. Did he say where he was going when he left Big Sur? Can you recall what brand of motorcycle he was riding? You once mentioned he'd been in the military in WW II. What branch?
Say hello to Mrs. Marx for me if you see her. By the way, did you ever really meet Henry Miller?

Love,
Carlisle

4

Once More, The Rider

The hum of rubber tires and trees passing by as if they were moving and Harry were standing still. It felt good again, the road, even if the stratus cloud formations were keeping things dark and sending down light rain.

At a state park just north of the Columbia River, Robert Kincaid stopped. His bad ankle had stiffened in the last two hours and needed exercise. Highway jumped down and sniffed grass and trees and picnic tables, hiking his leg to mark territory he would never see again.

Kincaid walked slowly across wet grass, reached down and massaged his ankle, walked some more until the ankle felt limber and almost normal. Fifteen minutes later he gave a low whistle, letting Highway know it was time to saddle up and leave. He opened the passenger door for the dog, allowing him to jump in, and went around to the driver's side, stepping easily into the truck in the long-legged way he had done for nearly three decades. If it were not for the damn ankle and the sudden dizzy spells that had begun coming on periodically in the last few months, Robert Kincaid would have felt about as good as he felt twenty years ago, and he was still hard and thin, the product of exercise and a conservative diet.

At first he ignored the dizziness, figuring it was a

recurrence of the thing he picked up in India years ago, a virus affecting the inner ear. During that episode, he spent four days in bed in a village south of Mysore, suffering vertigo, unable to stand, and crawling to a hole in the floor that served as a toilet.

Two months ago a Seattle physician had shoved his hands in the pockets of his lab coat and looked at Robert Kincaid sitting on the examination table. Kincaid hadn't been to a doctor since he broke his ankle nine years before.

"I can't say for sure what's causing your dizziness. Possibly labyrinthitis, which is what you may have had in India. However, that problem seems to have passed years back, and your current symptoms come and go, which leads me to think it's more likely a problem with your circulatory system. For a man of your age, your weight's good and your overall physical condition seems excellent, but for god's sake, man, stop the bloody smoking. That's the first thing. Any pain accompanying your dizziness?"

"Not too much," said Kincaid. "Sometimes a little discomfort in my chest."

"There are a number of tests we can run that would bring us closer to pinpointing your problem. You might be suffering from a form of angina, which is not a disease itself, but rather a set of symptoms, often presaging a heart attack caused by an underlying disease."

Robert Kincaid buttoned his shirt and thanked the doctor.

"So, what are we going to do?" asked the doctor.

"Nothing," replied Robert Kincaid. "I shouldn't

have bothered you."

"Nothing? I can probably help, but I need the results of more tests."

Robert Kincaid had no money for further tests and no interest in them, either. As far as he was concerned, life came and life went. It was short for some, longer for others, and the true path lay somewhere between sniveling fear and a kamikaze plummet.

During his World War II days as a combat photographer in the Pacific, he came near to dying several times. On his wall at home was a photograph of Marines coming off a landing craft at Betio Island, in the Tarawa Atoll, November 1943, shortly after 9:00 in the morning. Following orders ("We want pictures of them coming ashore, goddamnit!"), Kincaid had been among the first of the first wave off the boats, leaping into the surf ahead of the assault troops. With his film in waterproof bags, his camera held high, he disembarked three hundred yards offshore, the Higgins boat hanging on a reef. They had been headed for Beach Red One. Most of them did not make it to the sand.

There had been the sound of machine guns and all around him geysers of water where rounds from mortars and 75-millimeter field guns were exploding. And the look on the faces in those photographs: the tight, puking fear of young men a long way from home, many of whom were about to die, rifles above their heads, wading into shore. On Betio, 291 acres of coral sand laced with concrete and coconut log bunkers, the Second Marine Division would suffer nearly three thousand casualties in three days. Near the end of that first day, Kincaid's assistant, a Nebraska farm boy who had been kneeling in the sand only two feet away and reloading a camera, had taken a sniper's bullet in the forehead and pitched backward without making a sound.

Leaving the physician's office, Kincaid walked to his pickup in the parking lot, climbed in, and lit a Camel. Leaning over the steering wheel, long gray hair mussed as usual, he said, "To hell with it," as he straightened up and started Harry. Then he recalled e. e. cummings's lines about doctors and other universes out there and, driving out of the parking lot, laughed softly to himself.

Robert Kincaid knew he was an anachronism, a creature out of his proper time. A vestige of what used to be, without function or purpose as things lay now. He subscribed to one technical photography magazine and a local newspaper, but television had always been an alien idea to him. While purchasing a new pair of jeans two years earlier, he stopped in the electronics section of a Seattle department store and for a few minutes watched a game show, which was being rendered simultaneously on thirty-two television sets of various sizes. Kincaid stood there blinking, as if he had been roused from a long sleep and awakened to the onslaughts of a foreign, yammering world.

A clerk approached the man in orange suspenders and politely asked if he was interested in buying a television, saying the twenty-five-inch console models were on sale at 20 percent off. Kincaid turned and blinked at the young man, feeling disoriented and as if the man speaking to him were connected by invisible wires to the television screens and had been sent by the machines themselves. Behind him the game-show audience began screaming something, apparently at the contestants.

The clerk glanced at the screens and said, "Sure can win a lot of money and stuff on those game shows."

Kincaid tried to conjure up something in reply, but couldn't. He hurried from the store, thinking how far it seemed from his days along the Great Ice in another lifetime with spear in hand and shivering in the cold. But that cold had been real and natural, not the chill he continually felt in the faces about him, in the roar of urban traffic. When he left the store, three young men were juking along the sidewalk, coming toward him. One carried a portable music contraption, while the other two carried speakers attached to the machine. The music was loud and unintelligible to Robert Kincaid. Going home to the island in Puget Sound where he lived, he stood in the bow of the ferry and let the bitter wind and rain come directly upon him.

～

In late afternoon, with the weather breaking, Robert Kincaid crossed the Columbia River at Astoria, Oregon. Under the long arch of bridge, river and ocean traffic moved back and forth on the water, the roll of big commerce below the wheels of a twenty-seven-year-old pickup named Harry.

"Rode a motorcycle north through here once,

Highway," he said to the dog sleeping on the seat beside him. Highway lifted his ears and looked quizzically at Robert Kincaid.

"That was in 1945. Bridge wasn't built then, had to take the ferry from Oregon to Washington. The bike was a sweet Ariel Square Four, smooth as a baby's skin from tickover up to decent touring speed. Bought it used with a chunk of my back pay when I came out of the Marines; wish I'd never sold it. I was coming up from Big Sur, looking for a place to land more or less permanently and get back to work. That was way before your time, Highway, and I was a lot younger then, a lot younger."

He found a small grocery store and bought fruit and bread, cheese and assorted vegetables, still existing on the simple, inexpensive diet that had sustained him for decades. The cashier was bored and focused her eyes on the ceiling while he counted out $4.63 in small change taken from his coffee can.

The manager of a third-rate motel, in wrinkled corduroys and flannel shirt and growing a three-day beard, said he didn't mind a dog in the room as long as it was well behaved. Kincaid assured him Highway was better mannered than most people.

The manager replied, "That ain't saying much, mister, and might even be an insult to your dog. Run a motel like this one for a while, and you get a pretty dim view of the human condition." He slid a key across the counter. "Number eight, through the front door and turn left."

Robert Kincaid, out on the road again and, except for his dog, alone as always. He and

Highway had their suppers in the room, neither speaking to the other while they ate. Crunch of dog food, slish of a knife through cheese. Later they walked along the waterfront and watched the river traffic, the retriever finding much of interest in rusty fuel barrels and coils of rope. Harry sat in a stretch of thirty parking spaces in front of the motel. There were no other vehicles in the lot.

Back in the room, Kincaid lay on the floor, brushing off Highway's attempts to lick his face. He did a series of leg lifts and followed them with thirty pushups. Afterward, a little short of breath, he stripped to T-shirt and shorts, rubbed Tiger Balm on his bad ankle, and slid into bed with *The Green Hills of Africa*. Highway flopped down on the floor next to where Kincaid had propped himself.

The bedspread had a hole in it. Kincaid lifted the spread, looked through the hole at a stain on the wallpaper, and returned to reading. Just as the bwana was approaching a salt lick in Africa, a light rapping on the door startled Kincaid and brought a growl from Highway. Kincaid got up and asked who was there.

"It's me, Jim Wilson, manager."

Kincaid pulled on his jeans and opened the door.

Jim Wilson held up two bottles of beer. "It's awfully slow tonight, thought you might like a late-evening beer and a little conversation. Or, if I'm bothering you, just tell me to go away, and I'll do that with no rancor involved." He glanced at the bed. "Oh, man, I'm sorry, looks like you were already tucked in."

"I was just reading a little." Kincaid swung open the door and patted the dog standing next to his leg. Highway was still mistrustful and giving off low guttural sounds. "Shssh, it's okay, boy."

Jim Wilson used a church key to open the beers and handed one to Kincaid. He put his back against the door and slid down it easylike until he was sitting on the worn carpet. Kincaid sat in the only chair in the room, a bit of a creaker featuring cracked maroon vinyl on the seat and back. Highway sat by the bed and stared at Wilson, then stretched out with his head on his paws, still watching.

The manager lifted his beer. "Here's to better days."

Kincaid raised his bottle a few inches in reply.

"Where you headed, if you don't mind me asking?"

"Oh, more or less wandering around here and there. Got a little cabin fever and decided just to get out and go down the road for a while." Kincaid took a sip of his beer and lit a Camel. Though he wasn't overly suspicious by nature, he had always been vague when people asked him where he had been or was going. It was the sort of caution one developed out in less settled parts of the world, where such information could be used in nefarious ways.

The manager asked if he could bum a cigarette, and Kincaid tossed him the pack and his Zippo lighter.

"Looks as if you've had this lighter for a long time," Wilson said, lighting his cigarette and running his thumb across the scratched surface of the

Zippo, noticing the initials RLK etched into the surface and barely readable.

"Bought it at the PX in Manila, back in the forties, when I was shipping out for home after the War."

"Well, I missed the big war by some years." He tossed the lighter and cigarettes back to Kincaid. "Grew up just in time for Vietnam. Could've missed that one, too, and it wouldn't have bothered me."

Jim Wilson looked tired, bags under his eyes with an overall slump to him, worn and stained like the motel carpet. Even though he was easily twenty-five years younger than Kincaid, he looked older. A heavy drinker, Kincaid guessed.

Wilson asked the first question all old soldiers ask of one another. "What outfit were you with?"

"Got bounced around a bit, Second Marines most of the time. Pacific. Combat photographer."

"No kidding. Never knew a combat photographer. Ran into a few in 'Nam, but never got to know them well. Some of them were pretty wild, took more chances than the grunts."

Kincaid said nothing, tugged on his beer.

"Made it through all right, huh?" Jim Wilson was looking at him. "No war wounds, anything like that?"

"I was lucky. No other word for it. Took a sliver of shrapnel in the left side, just under my ribs. That was on Betio. Came in, went out a couple of inches later. The medics had worse problems than my scratch, so they dumped sulfa in the holes, patched me up in all of five minutes, and went on down the beach with their morphine and tourniquets. I was okay after a week or so. Didn't even get a Purple Heart."

Kincaid chuckled, and without thinking about it rubbed his hand over the old wound, feeling the scars beneath his T-shirt.

The manager straightened his legs in front of him, then pulled up a knee and rested his arms on it, bottle of beer dangling from his right hand. "Hell, I was in supply, so 'Nam wasn't all that tough for me, hanging around Saigon playing volleyball and avoiding social diseases where possible, serving my time and counting the days. Damn, though, some of the grunts took an awful licking out in the bush. Guess it wasn't all that pretty out where you were, either."

"No, wasn't pretty at all. If the Japanese didn't nail you, malaria and about a thousand other tropical bad things did. It was really tough going for some of the boys, really tough. Coming up those beaches with the enemy dug in tight and hard, and the only thought being how to get off the beach and into cover. Got to remember, these were guys who'd been car salesmen, farmers, auto mechanics, only a little while before."

"How'd you feel about Harry S. Truman dropping the bomb on 'em?"

Kincaid paused, looked at his beer, looked at Jim Wilson. "Some of us, a lot of us, had been out there for three years. Certain photographers and journalists like war; something to do, I guess, with proving your mettle, setting up more or less artificial risks for yourself...I don't know what it is, for sure.

But I never discovered any romance in the whole business."

He took a long swallow of beer. "The Japanese were tough soldiers. Me, I had no interest in riding the Sea of Japan into the teeth of the Empire. I just wanted to come home and get away from the dying. So did a lot of the other guys, most of them, whatever it took."

Kincaid shrugged and focused on some indiscernible point above Jim Wilson's head, letting the evasiveness of his answer mingle with the smoke from their cigarettes.

He went on, voice slightly above a whisper. "I came home, bought a motorcycle, rode it down to Big Sur and back up the coast through here, just trying to get it all out of my mind. You never really do, though. The images stay sharp and clear. And the smells, cordite and gangrene, diesel fumes and burning oil and coral dust. Heading toward those beaches in amphibious vehicles, hanging up on the reefs way out from shore, and knowing there wasn't anything to do but go into the water and wade in. Ducks on the pond, as we used to say."

Jim Wilson decided to get off war and on to something else. "Big Sur's real pretty. Went down there a few times when I was teaching at the University of San Francisco. Lots of tourists in motor homes making those hairpin curves on Route 1. Must have been quite a bit different when you visited, pretty laid back."

"Yeah, it was. Couldn't have been more than a hundred or so people living there on a permanent basis. Quite a few people passing through from all over, though. Lots of 'em claiming to be artists and musicians. Never saw or heard much art. Aside from a handful apparently doing serious writing and other things, there seemed to be a lot of talk about art, but not much in the way of actually doing it. The permanent residents mostly seemed to be scrabbling around trying to survive. I was only there a few days, however, so I could have picked up the wrong impression."

It might have been the beer, might have been the evening or the simple need to talk with another human being, to say things long interred and never spoken that caused Robert Kincaid to go on. Strangers are safe in that way, and Jim Wilson would be left behind in the morning, still a stranger and lacking other pieces required to complete a whole that Kincaid kept to himself. Except for Francesca Johnson, who knew most of what there was to know, Kincaid had always left only a small piece of himself before pushing on.

He brushed back his hair with both hands and stared at the floor for a moment, then looked again at Jim Wilson. "Met a young woman there, in Big Sur, a cellist. I carried her cello down to a deserted beach. We walked north a mile or so, along the water and around a headland. She said the tide would come in and we'd be trapped on that particular beach and couldn't get back around the headland until low tide. But I didn't care, and she didn't care. She never asked me about the war. Her brother had been killed in Italy during the taking of Salerno, so she knew something about the pain and fear.

"We stayed there for a long time, her playing

cello, waves crashing in and seabirds calling, shadows from the sea stacks moving across the water and onto the beach as the day went down. Her name was Wynn, I remember. Kind of a pretty girl in an unusual way, not much more than twenty, if that, and blazing with life. I recall lying there on the sand, listening to her play, Schubert I think she said it was, and remembering everything I'd seen in the last few years and working on forgetting it at the same time.

"Kept thinking some of the water washing up twenty yards away might have been the same water we rode on going into Tarawa and other places. I don't know how long she played, or how long I lay there with a bottle of red wine and thought and tried not to think all at the same time. After a while, when the sun was about gone, she leaned the cello against a rock and sat down beside me on the sand…I've always remembered how warm the sand was, and how she leaned back, rested on her arm and looked down at my face. I built a fire out of driftwood, and we stayed there all night."

Wilson recognized there was a kind of therapy going on in the shabby motel room, that this man, Kincaid, was trying to engage in more than idle storytelling. Just what he was doing wasn't clear, but there was a kind of essential reaching back, late in a man's life. Some necessary recounting of an important moment, maybe for no other reason than re-inscribing memories, like aborigines around a camp fire keeping alive the old tales and legends.

"Sounds as if she was an interesting woman."

Kincaid reached for his beer and bumped the

lampshade with the movement of his hand. Quick shadows wobbled across the room, and Highway looked up in alarm. Kincaid touched the shade to settle it.

"We talked about me staying on in Big Sur, and I gave it some thought, but there seemed to be a whole world waiting out there to look at. My heart was full of all I wanted yet to do, to see, to experience. Coming out of the war I was a spring, wound tight as hell, a long way from any kind of center within myself, had this sense of my life going by and a lot of things to see and do yet."

"So you left after a few days?"

"Yes. That was pretty quick, I know. There was a moment when I was saddled up and standing by the motorcycle, when she was looking at me and had her fingers hooked in one of my belt loops, that I really did lean against the leaving. I rode out of there ten minutes later, but it didn't have the sense of a real ending. I figured we'd stay in touch, see each other again. We said we would and meant it at that instant, I suppose. Like all those things usually turn out, though, time and distance got in the way. I wrote her two or three times, telling her I'd decided to settle up in the Seattle area and was looking for a place.

"But she'd apparently gone on to somewhere else, and I was moving around a lot back then, so, if she wrote me, our letters probably just got absorbed by the post office, ended up in a dead box. She had a pretty good sense of herself and was a real independent woman for her age and times, so I'm guessing she's done all right. Back then she wasn't any more ready for something permanent than I was.

"God, that was a whole other lifetime." Robert Kincaid paused and took a deep breath, let it out slow. "You said you were a university professor?"

"Yeah, taught psychology for nine years. Couldn't stand the academic life, if you can call it a life. A gaggle of socialists preaching solemn philosophies about equality while protecting about the most rigid class structure of any social or professional group you'll find. Quit and just bummed around for a few years. Ended up running this motel. Don't know how long I'll stay at it, though."

Jim Wilson, motel manager, stood up and stretched. "Better turn in, myself; plumbing's busted in unit six, so fixing it'll take up most of tomorrow morning. Good talking to you. And you're right about your dog, what you said about him having more polish than most humans. He can check in here anytime, with or without you." He stretched his hand toward Robert Kincaid.

"Good luck. Been nice talking to you." Kincaid shook Wilson's hand and closed the door behind him. After returning to bed and picking up the book, Kincaid discovered the big bwana was now looking at rhino tracks by the salt lick and was getting ready to blow away one or more miscellaneous critters. He put down the book and turned off the bedside lamp.

Later, as he slept and dreamed a strange dream, and it was part remembrance and part fantasy and having something to do with talking to a seaman in the old Raffles Bar in Singapore, his arm dangled off the bed. Highway licked the hand that accidentally had reached down and touched him.

Outside, a ship named the *Pacific Vagabond* came under the bridge and headed for its berth. Among the items stacked in its cavernous hold was a shipment of television sets from Korea, which had been offloaded in the Pacific and transferred to another ship at the modern port facilities in Tarawa.

5

The Search

South Dakota lay in deep autumn, and on a windy, gray morning, the rural mail carrier stopped at a box labeled *Carlisle McMillan, Route 3*. Fifty yards up the dirt lane, Carlisle was carrying lumber around a corner of what was still called old man Williston's place. In the enduring custom of rural America, places kept the name of the first person who had built on the land.

The mail carrier saw Carlisle and honked to let him know a letter had arrived. The McMillan fellow didn't get much mail, so it seemed a good idea to notify him that his box contained something for a change. Carlisle looked up, waved, and walked down the lane, while the mail carrier went on north toward Axel and Earlene Looker's farm. Axel would probably be leaning on his mailbox, the carrier thought, waiting for his crop subsidy check. He had been in that exact place for the last two days and complained about the inefficiencies of the damn government whenever his check arrived late.

While rebuilding old man Williston's house, Carlisle acquired a partner. A big tomcat drifted by halfway through the project and decided to stick around. Carlisle studied the long-haired tabby with a torn left ear and yellow eyes. The cat studied Carlisle and stayed for lunch and then for supper and eventually decided a permanent residence was in order.

"Well, big guy, I think the name Dumptruck suits you," Carlisle said on the fifth day. "So if you don't mind, we'll leave it at that." Dumptruck blinked. Carlisle grinned.

Dumptruck was sitting on the porch railing when Carlisle walked back from the mailbox. They both went inside, Dumptruck heading for his favorite place under the wood stove, Carlisle pouring a cup of tea from the battered pot he had picked up at the Goodwill Store in Falls City. He rested the cup on the extension table of his radial arm saw, which had been set up in the living room for the last three months while he detailed the house.

The letter was from his mother, Wynn, whom he had written only ten days earlier. Fast turnaround for Wynn, since she tended to lose mail and paychecks and doctors' prescriptions. Though, to her credit, she could remember the important things, such as complicated passages in Schubert's works and obscure details in the history of sculpture.

November 20, 1981

Dear Carlisle,

Gosh, you have a mailbox and everything. That sounds awfully settled, for you. I enjoyed hearing about the old place you bought and are fixing up. Maybe I can get out there to see it sometime. Anyway, I'm happy for you.

Any interesting women in your life? Sorry about that question, but mothers, even a strange one such as

I, think about those things. It's hard for me to believe you're going to be forty in a few years, and I would-n't mind a grandchild or two, you know.

Now, about the questions in your last letter, con-cerning your father and what I can remember of him. I can only repeat what I've said before. He had been in the military, worked as a photographer before the war and also in the Pacific during the war, and recently had been discharged from (I think) the Marines. He didn't seem to want to talk about the war very much. In fact, my feeling was he didn't want to talk about it at all. Robert was his first name, his last is completely gone from my memory, if I ever knew it at all.

I met him in late September of 1945, the same day Bela Bartok died. His motorcycle was red with chrome on certain parts. On the gas tank was a logo, silver-colored, that had the name of the motorcycle, and all I remember is that the name started with an "A." Memory is such an imperfect thing and so darned selective. I once filled the gas tank for him, stood there and stared at the logo, but I can only see the first letter. And yet I can still remember a story he told me about meeting a sailor in Singapore. Odd, isn't it?

Other things. He wore a bracelet, on his right wrist, I think. He was tall and thin and dressed sim-ply, wore suspenders. Though I can no longer recall the details of his face, my sense of it is that he was not particularly handsome, not the reverse, either. But that ordinary continuum does not really apply, because there was something distinctive about him, kind of an unusual-looking man. One thing I do remember is his eyes and how they looked. Old eyes, as if he were far older than whatever age he was (he must have been somewhere in his early thirties).

Now what? It all seems like such an old while-ago, and I was so young, just nineteen and rebellious as an unbroken filly, all kinds of nutty dreams about the artistic life and living close to nature. But I still can see him. He was letting his hair grow after leaving the military, and he tied it back with a blue bandana when he rode his motorcycle. As I said, he wasn't all that good-looking in the way we've come to define handsome, but he nonetheless cut quite an attractive figure in his leather jacket, jeans and boots, and sunglasses as we rode across the high bridges of Big Sur.

Let me know how your house-building project is going. All is calm here. Come visit me sometime. In spite of everything, I still remember your father as a lovely, warm man, even though we were together only three or four days. I am not sorry about anything, for he gave me you.

Love,
Your Mother, Wynn

P.S. I saw Mrs. Marx the other day and gave her your regards. She said to say hello to you and still thinks of you as she would a son, always talking about Cody and you. Drop her a note sometime. Dear ol' Jonathan, your beloved stepfather for six of your younger years, stopped by on his way up the coast from San Francisco. We went for coffee, and he told me about his trust fund, his novel he was trying to get *published, and his two most recent wives. He asked me out for dinner, but I said no, thanks. Wonder what I ever saw in him?*

Carlisle McMillan took out a sheet of paper and dug a carpenter's pencil from his shirt pocket. Pretty sparse list, he thought, but wrote down all the clues Wynn had given him:

First name "Robert"
Motorcycle starting with "A"
Bracelet?
WW II-Pacific. Marines?
Photographer before and during the war
Singapore = traveled a lot?
Age = Early thirties

That list could be the rows of a table. Across the top, the columns, he could enter names as he came by them and search for matches between the names and the clues. But where to start? He needed an angle of entry, but couldn't come up with anything except what might be a never-ending search through old magazines and newspapers.

Carlisle sat quietly, thinking, and jumped a little when the phone rang. It was Buddy Reems, his partner in crime from the housing development days in Oakland. Something of a wild man, but a decent carpenter and genuinely good person overall.

"Carly, you ol' snake, good to hear your voice. Your mother gave me this number. What the hell are you doing and where are you? Wynn said something about the Dakota south of the north one. Is that on maps? Can you get there from here? Need some kind of interplanetary passport just to enter?"

Carlisle laughed. Buddy hadn't changed. When they'd split two years ago, Buddy had gone off to join a commune in New Mexico.

"Where are you, Buddy?"

"Oakland. Back to building crap and drinking myself near to death on weekends trying to forget all the bad work I did the previous week. I hear you've built yourself a house or fixed up an old one or something like that."

Carlisle told him about the project on the Williston place. Said it had come along pretty nice, well enough that word had passed around and led to work in a couple of nearby towns.

"How's the women situation? Doing any serious construction along those dimensions, or is it just virgins and prisoners they send out there?"

"Couple of possibilities. I've been seeing a woman who works at a local cafe. Hey, Buddy, what happened to your great ideals of communal living?"

"Christ, what a joke that was, Carly. You may recall I went down there because of this girl. Remember? I wrote and told you she had legs longer than last month. Even offered to share her with you if you'd come down."

Carlisle shook his head, smiling. He remembered Buddy's letter about the girl and how that commune thing was going to be the best deal ever.

"Yeah, I remember. So what happened?"

"Well, as it worked out, the girl ran off to another commune with a guitar player who was turning on with all sorts of chemical shit and kept singing old songs from the sixties about flowers and peace and free love. The last part was all that interested me. The other half of it was that I was the only person in the whole deal with any skills. So they had me building army-style kitchens and mess halls and dormitories while everyone else was sitting around smokin' dope and talking about…how do you pronounce it, Neats-key?…German guy, anyway. Some philosopher or something."

"How about NE-cha, Friedrich Nietzsche."

"Yeah, that's it. I hate you college kids, Carly. If you weren't the best carpenter I've ever seen, I wouldn't have anything to do with you. Well anyway, you can imagine how all that Neats-key and peace/love/flowers junk went down with me, so I pulled out right after the girl escaped with the flower-power guitar man. I didn't even say adios, neither did she. He wasn't worth a damn on the guitar, either. Remember when we used to go down and hear Jesse Lone Cat Fuller? Mister peace and love couldn't have clipped the loose ends of Jesse's new guitar strings."

The conversation went on that way and eventually Carlisle mentioned his search for his father. Buddy, for all his wild talk and equally wild behavior, was a practical man when there was a problem to be solved. And, as usual, he was confident in his ability to deal with such matters.

"Let me plow around here for you, maybe up in

Sacramento. I'm leaving for there in about an hour, going to visit a woman I met at a Fleetwood Mac concert last month. She ain't the prettiest thing in the world, but knows how to use her body like a table saw."

Carlisle smiled. The same Buddy, hustling, never without movement or words, even in his early forties.

"I know a couple of guys in Sacramento who might have access to motor vehicle records. Christ, it was more than thirty years ago, but the damn bureaucrats keep everything forever, so there could be something there. Okay, I'm writing this down. First name, Robert. Right? His bike started with the letter "A." Bought it right after World War II, maybe August or September of 1945 or sometime around there. Wonder how many motorcycles were sold in the Bay Area right after the War—two, maybe three, kazillion."

"I'm not sure he bought it right after the war. Maybe he had it in storage while he was gone."

"Oh good, Carly. That narrows it down to about half of all the bikes ever sold anywhere. But I'll give it a shot. Stuff that old won't be on computers. Hand digging. I'll give it a whirl, though. You say she works at a local restaurant?"

"Who?"

"The woman you're gunning, that's who."

"Yep, but I'd hardly call it 'gunning.' Place called Danny's Cafe. Best hot turkey sandwiches between Omaha and Cheyenne. Lots of gravy and mashed potatoes."

"Sounds good to me. Hot turkeys and pretty

women, or is it the other way around? Anyway, I'll be in touch. One more thing, Carly. Don't die dumb. That's my new motto."

"What?"

"I'm making a list of ways I don't want to die and avoiding situations where those ways might happen to me."

"For example?"

"Don't die in a hospital, don't let that happen. That's first, and it's basic. Better to fall off a roof instead, just as you nail down the last shingle on the best house you've ever built. A second dumb is being tail-ended by a rusty '68 Cadillac with bald tires, in front of Kmart while a blue-light special on men's underwear is commencing."

Carlisle was laughing, missing Buddy Reems and his craziness, sometimes.

"Here's one more: being hit by flying debris from a rotary lawn mower operated by an over-weight sixty-four-year-old Rotarian in a planned retirement community. That's all I've worked up so far, but I'll have more. I'll send you the complete list sometime. Take care, Carly. Great talking to you. I'll let you know if I find anything."

"Thanks, Buddy. Same to you. I appreciate your help."

Seven hours later, Buddy called again. Roar of traffic in the background.

"Carly, me. I'm in a phone booth in Sacramento. Nice young thing named Nancy at the motor vehicles bureaucracy of records helped me out. Not all that easy, but easier than I thought. Took three hours of digging and sorting, but we found a few things. Are you ready with paper and pencil? Twenty-eight honchos having the first name Robert registered motorcycles in San Francisco in August and September of 1945. Lots of Harleys and Indians, but only one machine starting with an 'A,' something called an Ariel Square Four, registered as a used bike on September 24, 1945. The 'Square Four' business probably has something to do with cylinder alignment and..."

Carlisle interrupted him. "Buddy, the name. Who registered it?"

"Oh yeah, the important stuff. I almost forgot. Name was Robert L. Kincaid. No address listed except general delivery, San Francisco. No phone number, either. Those would probably be no use, anyway, too old, thirty-six years ago."

"Spell the last name for me."

Carlisle carefully printed the name as Buddy spelled it.

"Gotta run, Carly. Ms. Table Saw awaits in my pickup only four feet away. Good luck, and let me know if there's anything else I can do on this end."

"Thanks again, Buddy. This might really help."

"No sweat. Bye-bye."

After finishing with Buddy, Carlisle immediately revised his list of clues:

First name "Robert"—last name might be "Kincaid," middle initial "L."

Motorcycle starting with an "A"—possibly Ariel Square Four.

He studied the list, went into the kitchen and pulled a beer from the fridge. Back at his trestle desk, he began to doodle.

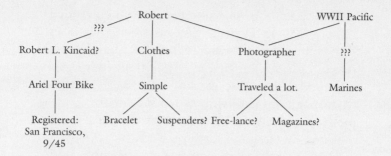

Clearly, all paths through the diagram were dead ends, except for the photographer category and possibly military records. He called his mother early the next morning and asked if she knew any old photographers with whom he might speak.

"Carlisle, does this have to do with your father?"

"Yes." He told her what Buddy Reems had discovered in Sacramento.

"Kincaid? I wish I could tell you that was his last name. But I simply cannot remember, if I ever knew. Though as I said before, I think he once told me. Are you sure you want to keep on with this, Carlisle? It might lead to great disappointment for you, maybe for both of us."

"Yes, I'm sure. C'mon, Wynn, think of a photographer I can talk to, someone who might know something about the history and development of photography in this country."

"Well, there's Frank Moskowitz, who lives in a cabin outside of town, up in the hills near Russian Gulch. He's in his seventies, I'd say, and seems to talk a good line when he comes into the gallery. His work is undistinguished, but he's still out there taking pictures. I'll look up his number for you."

She gave him the number and then added, "There's an incident I've never told you about. Why, I don't know. It didn't come to mind, I guess, till you got me thinking about all this. Your father and I rode his motorcycle down the coast to a place where sea lions gathered. When we got there, two men were using a rifle to shoot at the seals, handing the gun back and forth between them.

"I was terribly distraught over the whole business. Your father told me to stay by the motorcycle and went down to where the men were shooting. He simply walked up to them, grabbed the rifle, and threw it into the ocean. After that, they shouted at him and obviously were very angry. One tried to start a fight, but your father never moved, just stood there and stared at them. After a while they walked down the beach and your father came back to where I was standing.

"I could see he was furious and asked him what he said to them. He replied, 'I just told them I'd seen enough senseless killing and if they wanted to make this into something more, I was going to throw them in right where I'd tossed the rifle because that wouldn't be senseless.' If I wasn't partially in love with him before, I was after that whole business with the seals."

They talked for a few more minutes. When they had finished, Carlisle immediately dialed the number she had given him. An old, gruff voice answered, "Moskowitz."

Carlisle introduced himself and asked about American photographers. Had Mr. Moskowitz ever heard of a photographer named Kincaid?

"Name seems familiar. Can't say for sure. If he's really well-known, he might be in *Who's Who*."

Carlisle hadn't thought of that and jotted it down.

"Mr. Moskowitz, if a photographer was doing a lot of traveling back in the thirties, who would he have been working for in those days?"

"Hard to say. There's always been a crowd of us out there wandering around on our own hook. Not many magazines in those days could afford to send someone overseas. Comes down to the biggies. You know, *Time, Life, Look, National Geographic,* those outfits."

Moskowitz seemed to drift off and began talking about camera equipment and film, about his frustrations in getting his own work published. Carlisle listened politely, and when the old man paused for breath, he thanked him for his help and said he had to go.

"Your mother's a fine lady, Mr. McMillan, a fine lady, even though she doesn't show my images in that gallery where she works."

"Well, who knows, Mr. Moskowitz. Maybe sometime."

"Yeah, maybe sometime," the old man said and hung up.

Carlisle stoked the wood stove and turned in for the night. As he angled down into sleep, the blow and howl of the wind outside sounded like the roar of a road bike coming around the long curves of Big Sur, a long time ago.

~

An hour past dawn, a slight chill in the air, Robert Kincaid checked out of the Oregon motel and booted Harry into life, listening to the engine. Something not right, damn choke again. He took a small toolbox from behind the seat and put on his light parka. Highway leaned out the window, trying to see around the hood as Kincaid raised it. Kincaid tweaked the choke screw and listened to the engine, nodded to himself, and gently re-fastened the hood.

Back in the truck. "Zen and the art of old pick-up maintenance, Highway. Not as romantic as Mr. Pirsig had us believe about working on motorcycles, in that book of his. Not much Zen under Harry's hood, that's for sure. Least none I can discover. But, then, trucks are not the same as bikes. Now Harry, here, is personal in his own way, but not like the feel of a good road bike under you. Should've kept that Ariel. Could've roped you on behind me and let those 500 cc's take us down the road."

Highway sniffed Kincaid's jacket for any unusual morning smells, found none, and lay in his place on the truck seat while Kincaid put on his reading glasses, studied a road map, and let the heater warm the cab and clear the windshield.

He decided to stay on Route 101, head down to northern California and then cut east. That would take him a little south of the Black Hills, but he could always turn north again or catch the Hills on his way home.

With the Pacific showing itself between low, green mountains, Robert Kincaid drove no more than forty-five along the winding coastal highway. Down hills, up hills, curves to the left and curves to the right, moving along on autopilot.

He tried to get back the essence of his night dream. While his body had rested, his mind was working its way back to Singapore when that island country was still raw and uncontrolled, a crossroads of the world. Pirates, soldiers of fortune, smugglers. Men with knives on their hips and maps in their pockets and plans shorn of morality even as they were formulated. The kind of world Robert Kincaid had dreamed about as a boy.

All the clichés that weren't yet clichés in those times. Overhead fans turning slowly in rough joints, and a woman named Juliet who wore a low-cut black dress and played good piano while she sang Kurt Weill songs. One night, two men nearly killed each other for the privilege of her attentions, though she played no part in encouraging the contest and, as it turned out, was interested in neither of them.

Kincaid remembered her, liked her music. He was in his late twenties, just getting out on the road and going to work, and the woman called Juliet was older, forty perhaps. Nothing transpired between them. At that age, he would have been afraid of such a woman and what she might have known that he didn't, about beds and such. He sat in the Raffles Bar, finished his beer, and looked down his glass as if it were a lens. Her image had been distorted but was still quite beautiful to his way of thinking. He wondered if she made it out before the Japanese swept down a few years later. Odds were, she had. People such as Juliet always made it out of wherever they needed to get out of. She, too, was a last cowboy of sorts.

Rolling south toward California, he started into a hum, a song Juliet had done every evening those forty-some years ago. "Sailor's Tango," he seemed to recall. And a face in the dream came back to him, but only a first name, Aabye. First mate on a ship called the *Moroccan Wind.* How in hell would I remember the name of the man's ship, Kincaid smiled to himself. Some things stick, others don't. They'd had a couple of beers together at the Raffles.

Aabye last-name-lost had talked about his great aspiration to own a schooner but knew he couldn't swing it financially. Robert Kincaid mentioned he had just finished a piece of photo work on the old China Sea schooner trade and devoted most of his attention to an aging captain who was nearing retirement and was looking for someone to keep the boat going. Kincaid told the man named Aabye that something might be worked out when it came to money, since the captain loved the fine boat so much. The schooner was called the *Paladin,* and Kincaid had directed the man to where it was docked. The mate had shaken Kincaid's hand and thanked him, then walked off to locate a schooner called the *Paladin.*

And those were the memories launched by the dream. Robert Kincaid had hundreds, thousands, of such memories. Moving south along the Oregon coast, he looked west toward Singapore and wondered if the man named Aabye had ever found a boat, there in the very last days of the schooner trade, and hoped he had. Wondering, always, about the Juliets and Aabyes, the Marías and Jacks, the others from his time out there in the world. He remembered them all with warmth and was grateful to them for the memories.

A lighthouse came up on his right, and he automatically framed it in his mind, considering a shot. He decided to let it go by; there were already too many photographs of lighthouses on sunny mornings.

He went on down the road, still thinking about the lighthouse, sorting possibilities. At a turnout where tourists could pull their Winnebagos over and get a snapshot of distant sea views, he stopped and searched through the rolls of Tri-X. Mixed in with the Tri-X was a single roll of Kodak Technical-Pan, rated at ASA 25, a slow film designed for copying line drawings and other graphics.

But the T-Pan had a singular characteristic. If exposed at a much faster speed and developed in an unorthodox fashion, it washed out virtually all intermediate gradations of tone and rendered the subject in stark black and white, making the subject fairly leap out at the viewer. He had used that technique in Scotland once, in the Isles of Glencoe. A small castle had sat a hundred yards offshore on an island just large enough to contain it, the castle's reflection pristine in the surrounding water. In the final print, the gray castle walls and turrets had gone stark white, the water around it black, and the photograph looked as if the castle were sitting on its own reflection. He might be able to handle the lighthouse in a similar fashion, but give the shot its own slant.

He drove back along the sea road, watching the lighthouse move through the imaginary frame in his mind, until it was correctly positioned for the shot. Pulling over, he took one of the Nikon F's from his knapsack and loaded the T-Pan. When Kincaid put on his vest and pulled out the tripod, Highway jumped from the truck and began his usual search-and-discover tactics, nose to the ground.

Kincaid gave one of the tripod legs a long-practiced nudge with his boot, and the legs splayed out. He adjusted the height automatically, knowing without thinking consciously about it where he wanted the camera to rest. He fastened the camera to the tripod and pulled a cable release from the right side-pocket of his vest.

Kincaid's mind was working again, getting back to the sorting and thinking, simultaneously synthesizing the shot and analyzing the technique required to make it. While he screwed the cable release into the Nikon, he let a smile come over his face, then laughed out loud. Highway looked at him, puzzled.

"Dog, I'm only laughing because I'm here doing what it is I do best and realizing I haven't been doing enough of it, lately." He could feel strength coming back into his body, the energy and power that had been latent during the last few years of depression and self-pity.

Robert Kincaid, one of the old image-makers, a consummate illusionist who had brought back his view of things to millions of book and magazine readers, was working again. He bent over, looked through the viewfinder, made minor adjustments in camera tilt, and was ready for the shot. He could see the castle in Scotland and mapped that image onto what he was now doing, calling up technical procedures and laying out his plan of attack.

As always, his test of whether or not to take a photograph was to imagine the shot framed and hanging on a wall. Was it something he could live with for months, years, without tiring of it? If yes, the shot was worth the film and effort. If no, he packed up and moved on.

He imagined the exact way he wanted the final print to look. Thought about what it would take in terms of development and printing to achieve that effect. Took out his incident light meter and got an initial reading. The shadow cast by the lighthouse was in high contrast to the white concrete of the building. A high-contrast shot with high-contrast film; care would be needed. Robert Kincaid dialed in the compensations on his camera. Overexpose slightly, get a little of the shadow detail and bring back the washed-out highlights when he developed the film, fix up the rest when he made the print. He thumbed the cable release, the reflex mirror clicked, and he knew the shot was likely a good one. Another, same settings, just to have an extra negative to play with.

Finished, he slung the camera over his shoulder and flipped the tripod upside down, loosening the legs and letting the tubes slide down into one another. He poured a cup of coffee from the Thermos in his truck, unwrapped a Milky Way, and sat on a rock, looking out over the Pacific while he rubbed Highway's ears and remembered the elderly couple with whom he stayed for almost two weeks while doing the work in Scotland. Their fiftieth anniversary had occurred while he was there, and the village had thrown a fine party with fiddles and bagpipes and much laughter. A young woman had tried to teach him a traditional dance, and all of them had laughed at his attempts to imitate a highland warrior's victory steps. Robert Kincaid had laughed, too.

He bought the elderly couple two china teacups and saucers as a present. For nine years after, they and he exchanged periodic letters until he heard no more from them. A neighbor of the couple eventually wrote to say both had died within two months of one another. The woman first, the man not long after. She from something not mentioned, her husband from nothing more than heartbreak, according to the neighbor.

A cloud bank had formed far out over the water, maybe twenty miles, but the sun was warm where Robert Kincaid sat, and he stayed there for a long time, chewing slowly on his candy bar, and how long he stayed he wasn't certain and didn't care.

6

Francesca

Another morning of another day in a life descending, and Francesca Johnson pulled on cowboy boots with rundown heels, making ready for her daily outing. She fastened up her long hair, tugged a beret over her head, and took her woolen coat down from a peg near the kitchen door. The lane up to her farmhouse was washboarded, and as she walked down it toward the main road, she made a mental note to have Tom Winkler bring his grader by and get the lane fixed up before winter. Once the deep Iowa frost set in, there would be no road repair until spring.

November, and the sunlight had moved from the heated orange of summer to a pallid yellow cast. But the day was windless so far, and her walk would be pleasant enough, even though the air had a bite to it.

Today, she turned right, heading for Roseman Bridge. For the first half mile, the road was deserted, on either side crops in from the stubbled fields a month ago and Iowa beginning to hunker down for another endless winter. A grain truck passed her, heading toward Winterset. The man driving it waved, and Francesca waved back. A few minutes later, she heard the sound of a vehicle behind her and stepped off the road to let it pass.

Floyd Clark, in his new Chevy pickup, slowed and stopped.

"Mornin', Frannie. How ya doin' these days?"

"Good morning, Floyd. Oh just fine, about the same, you know. Putting up plastic over the north windows, caulking others. Getting the house ready for another winter." She hoped that Floyd wasn't going to use this opportunity to ask her out again.

"Well, if you need any help liftin' and such, me and son Matt'll be glad to come over and give you a hand. He's got a strong back, unlike the rest of us older folks that have spent our lives trying to pick up more than we should've."

Francesca thanked him and knew he spoke the truth. Back problems were endemic among farmers of rural Iowa. There was always something heavy that needed to be moved, right away it seemed, and nobody around to help. So they'd do it themselves and suffer the consequences. Richard's back had troubled him for the last ten years of his life.

Another example, she thought, of desire besting judgment, something about which she knew all too well. But then, she understood the reverse also, and who was to say where truth rested in such matters.

Floyd was fidgeting, fooling with the side mirror on his truck. She thought about targets of opportunity down the line he could use to invite her out, such as the New Year's dance at the Legion.

There was nothing wrong with Floyd Clark, but nothing specially right about him, either. Her feelings summed to no more or less than that, and she simply preferred not to form a relationship with him, however casual and harmless it might be. It wasn't the fact that talk would run through the cafes ("I see Floyd Clark's courtin' Frannie Johnson. Don't blame him. She's still quite a looker for her age, and Marge damn near talked him to death while she was still alive." "I dunno, Arch, something not right about Missus Johnson, something different about her, and I can't say what it is for sure, like she's not part of the rest of us"). Francesca, quite simply, wasn't interested and was trying to be gentle about it.

She decided to run an intercept by telling a partial lie. "Maybe I'll escape the cold for a while this year. Michael has invited me to Florida for the holidays. Sounds pretty good to me, so I think I'll take him up on it." Michael hadn't invited her yet, but he would. She had gone once before, and once had been enough. The grandchildren were fun, but all the artificial holiday spirit had made her uneasy, and Michael's new wife, his second, had been a little cool toward her.

Floyd Clark's face sagged almost imperceptibly, but he recovered. "Well, can't blame you for that. Me and Marge spent several winters in Brownsville, Texas, and were darned glad to get out of the cold for a while."

Francesca remembered Marge Clark going on and on about their snowbird winters in Texas. The organized activities, the shuffleboard and golf tournaments, the square dances and cocktail parties put together by the Brownsville Chamber of Commerce.

She said nothing back to Floyd, looked down at her boots, and the silence between them grew to uncomfortable proportions.

"Well," he said finally. "Best be gettin' on home and make sure Matt hasn't mortgaged the farm to finance one of his never-endin' expansion schemes. You gonna hold on to your land, Frannie?"

"Oh, I think so, Floyd. I haven't given a thought to selling it, even though I have about one call a week from some realtor wanting me to put it on the market. Land prices are awful high at the moment, I guess."

She didn't mention her reasons for staying on the land, for staying in Madison County. She did not say that maybe somewhere out there was a man named Robert Kincaid who might someday come looking for her. It was a romantic, starry-eyed hope, the sort of thing in which young girls engaged, but she clung to it nonetheless.

"Yep, land's goin' out'a sight. The two-hundred-forty next to us is for sale, and maybe young Matt's right, tellin' me all the time we ought to buy it just for investment purposes. Like he says, they ain't makin' any more of it."

Francesca smiled, not in affirmation but rather to indicate she was listening. She was also bored and wished Floyd would shift gears and move on.

A moment later he did. "Take care, Frannie. See ya' around."

"Goodbye, Floyd. Thanks for stopping and saying hello."

"Anytime. Always nice to see your smilin' face."

Floyd Clark steered the Chevy along ruts in the frozen mud, jouncing away from her and off toward son Matt's expansion plans. As it eventually turned out, he would give in and agree with Matt, after which they would pay nearly twice what the two-hundred-forty was worth in terms of intrinsic crop value. In another eighteen months, Iowa land prices would decline by 40 percent, as a rough time in the Midwest lofted itself, and Floyd would blame local bankers for getting him into the mess.

Not long after her talk with Floyd, Francesca rounded a curve and could see Roseman Bridge. And the heart of her always rose and fell at this moment. She remembered coming around the curve in a truck named Harry, when August was in high form and the sun beat upon the land, when a man named Robert Kincaid had come into her life only minutes before.

She remembered how he smiled when he first saw the bridge, and said, "It's great. A sunrise shot." And how he walked along the road, knapsack slung over his shoulder, and surveyed the bridge, planning how he would photograph it. And she remembered the clutch of black-eyed Susans he picked for her as thanks for showing him the bridge.

And later on there had been iced tea in the kitchen and easy talk about his life, about her life. And cold beer from his cooler, then vegetable stew she cooked, and a walk in the pasture when supper was through. Brandy and coffee after that.

Roseman Bridge stood silent on a November morning turning bleak, a northwest wind kicking up and rustling brown thistles and what leaves remained of autumn. The bridge was colored in peeling gray and faded red and leaned even more than it had in 1965, as if it were trying to reach the water beneath it. It seemed to be dying a slow death after all its hundred years of living, and apparently nobody cared that it was dying.

Middle River ran shallow and clear in this season, just before it would give up and freeze over for the winter. It gurgled and foamed around the rock where Robert Kincaid had stood and looked up at Francesca Johnson as she peered through a crack in the siding.

Some things endure, she thought, rocks and rivers, old covered bridges. Some things don't, hot August nights and all they bring, and we go on without them and eventually die and leave no mark of ourselves or of the depraved and valued sister that shared the same mind and body as an Iowa farm wife.

She smiled when she remembered a story Robert Kincaid had told her. He had been under another bridge in another time, in his knee-high rubber boots, using a wide-angle lens to give the bridge a sense of running into the distance above him. When he finished the shot, his boots had been stuck deep in the mud. He lost his balance and began falling backward, holding the camera up to protect it. Splat, he went, flat on his back into the mud with his boots still standing upright in the muck.

"So, there I was, lying in the mud, looking up at the sky and laughing at myself. I walked out in my stocking feet and washed off further upstream. Got the shot, though. That's all that ever matters."

She remarked to him about how easily he could laugh at himself. He had done that several times during their days together.

Kincaid had smiled and said, "I've always figured there are two main indicators of maturity. One is the ability to laugh at yourself. Most people take themselves and their lives a lot more seriously than circumstances call for, have trouble seeing the ultimate absurdity of the whole business. I keep myself amused by laughing at all the dumb things I do. And I do a lot of them, so I'm pretty well entertained most of the time."

Francesca had asked him what he thought to be the other sign of maturity.

"The ability to grin in admiration at others' accomplishments, instead of sulking in envy," he said without hesitating. "I recall the first time I ever heard Bach, and my immediate reaction was to grin. Afterward, I remembered my reaction better than what piece was playing, felt good about it, and I've tried to maintain that outlook. Sat in a cafe in Paris once, before the War, and listened to a guitar player, gypsy fellow named Django Reinhardt, who had only two workable fingers—lost the use of the other two in a fire—but still played with unbelievable speed and purity. I had the same reaction then. Admiration, not envy."

He held up his left hand with the ring and little fingers curled toward his palm, wiggling his thumb and other two fingers as if playing the guitar. "Somewhere in my files I have a shot of Django Reinhardt leaning against a building, smoking a cigarette, trenchcoat over his shoulder. Just two fingers and a thumb. Unbelievable.

"Then there are the photographs of the Mexican

Revolution by some shooter whose name I don't know, working with equipment and film a hell of a lot more primitive than what I have. Great pictures, incredible work. The sculptures done by Theodore Roszak, Picasso's stuff, all the rest. Instead of feeling envious, you just smile and go on and try to do better in your own work. Compete against your own limitations instead of worrying about what imperfections you can find in the accomplishments of others. Doesn't work that way for most people though; they seem to do the opposite. I guess because doing is a lot harder than whining."

He paused, smiled again. "Ask someone who lives alone as much as I do a simple question, and you get a lecture back, more than you ever needed to know about whatever it was you asked about in the first place. Sorry."

These sixteen years later, Francesca placed her hand on the left side of the bridge, where she had left the note for him. *If you'd like supper again when 'white moths are on the wing,' come by tonight after you're finished. Anytime is fine.*

God, what had possessed her to do that, she wondered, as she had wondered so many times. The risk, the one great roll of wicked dice in an otherwise blameless life. The parting of the robe as that depraved and valued sister came forth and took her place for those four days of a drama so oddly concentrated and yet never resolved.

Ah, she smiled to herself, but I would do it again with him, because of him. My great sin, I suppose, is that, except for a moment here and there, I have felt no contrition and never will.

The flight of a pigeon from its roost inside the bridge startled her. She took her hand from where she touched the old wood and began the long walk home, her steps like much of her life had been, a cadence so measured it had made her sometimes want to scream. In his own way, Robert Kincaid had helped her silence the scream, and she had been able to make do afterward.

7

The Elegance of Whimsy

Robert Kincaid drifted south through Oregon, following the coast. He had made the drive several times, though not for the last seven or eight years, and this stretch of America once again seemed fresh to his eye.

In Coos Bay, men were unloading a freighter, and Kincaid used his 200-millimeter lens to catch a longshoreman reaching high and guiding a cargo net. In Bandon, a fusty woman had combed the beaches for decades and displayed her keepings in and around and on top of a small frame building. She was somewhere in her eighties, with grayed hair sprouting at all angles, and carrying the harsh evidence of years in salt wind. But she had the energy and sparkle of someone much younger.

She saw Kincaid poking around outside, where at least fifty buoys of various faded colors hung from a picket fence. "C'mon in here, fella, and look around. Got lots of good stuff you could take home as souvenirs."

She had bottles from Australia, seawashed onto the coast by storms and tides. And pieces of driftwood overlaid with net fragments. A slice of a fishing boat's hull rested against her porch railing on which lay the handle of a shattered oar. A shark's tooth hung by a string from the oar handle. The tally seemed endless and probably approached that, though outside of certain constructs in physics and mathematics and human feelings, few things truly are of that degree.

Kincaid noticed how late morning sunlight caught a casual grouping of various-size bottles in one of her windows and asked if he might photograph them. She told him it was all right as long as he didn't bust nothin', and busied herself with cleaning seashells.

He studied the bottles. The light came through a cut glass jar on a shelf and was refracted onto a large green bottle, after which it bent again and entered a slim wine flask with Italy 1940 engraved on one side. The overall effect was a series of prisms mixing sunlight with the various colors of glass. No still-life photographer with all the time and control of a sophisticated studio could have arranged them better, and the elegance of whimsy had always fascinated Kincaid. The beauty of caprice, as he called it. Such patterns were everywhere if you knew how to see them. It took Kincaid fifteen minutes to set up the shot and twenty seconds to execute the mechanical aspects of firing the shutter and winding on the film.*

After repacking his equipment, Kincaid asked the woman what she might want for the Italian wine bottle. She squinch-eyed him in his plain

---

*Author's note: Kincaid's photograph of the bottles eventually was purchased by a collector and, in 1993, was loaned to the San Francisco Museum of Fine Arts for a show titled, "American Photography: Errant Lives and Unexpected Finds."

clothes and said two dollars would catch it all right. She rolled bubble wrap around the bottle and fastened it with tape.

"Got some awful nice whale vertebrae out back if you like that sort of thing."

Kincaid thanked her, but said his present need for whale vertebrae was limited and went on down the road, heading south along the sea.

Gold Beach came up, at the mouth of the Rogue River. He photographed a half-sunken boat, using five more frames of his Technical-Pan film. A man stopped by to talk, said he was delivering supplies to a tourist restaurant upriver, and if Kincaid wanted to ride along and keep him company, the man would stand him lunch. Highway evidenced a certain lack of confidence about the speedboat, but Kincaid lifted him in and they roared off, the dog's ears blowing and discernible terror in his eyes. Three hours later they were back at the mouth of the Rogue. Kincaid found a motel by the water and was on the road early the next morning.

By late afternoon, he was well into northern California and moving through timber country. Mendocino came up in another half-hour, in some ways—the ways of weathered roofs and picket fences and flowerbeds lined with stones and driftwood—a New England fishing village transported to the West Coast. It lay tranquil on a small peninsula jutting into the Pacific, with redwood forests running along Highway 1 on the landward side.

Kincaid stopped at a Chevron station on Main Street and gassed the pickup. He did a walk-around of Harry and was troubled by the look of the left front tire. The station attendant checked the tire and said it was ten pounds low.

"Might have a slow leak. Want me to look at it?"

Kincaid said yes and walked idly up Main Street, glancing into shop windows. Books and antiques and two bars, several cafes and a number of art galleries. He turned north on Kasten and stopped to look at a display of photography in a gallery window. The photographer's name was Heather Michaels. Her work was conventional, but well crafted, with a concentration on black-and-white landscapes. The grain and detail told him that Heather Michaels worked with a large-format camera, probably a 4 x 5.

Robert Kincaid stood there, hands in his pockets, and studied the photographs. Highway sat by his right leg and looked at Kincaid looking at whatever was in the window. Inside, a slim woman in her mid-fifties, wearing a long gray skirt, white blouse buttoned at the neck, and black shawl, was talking to a customer. Kincaid could not see her clearly through the glass, and she was standing in profile to him, but something in the way her long hair was fastened up and how she used her hands to emphasize the virtues of a piece of artwork caught his attention. Some flicker of recognition came into his mind, left him, came back again. Some featherlike tickle along the cambers of his memory. Where? When? The long hair, the almost musical gesticulations of her hands.

The woman changed position, showing her customer another piece of work. He could see more of her face, though reflections from the glass still muddled her image slightly.

Inside, Wynn McMillan glanced past the customer to whom she was talking and saw a curious-looking man at the window. The general sense of him was what first caught her attention. He was old, but not old at the same time. Tall and thin, wearing jeans and khaki shirt and suspenders. Unusual characters of all sorts moved through Mendocino, but there was something about this man that was far out of the ordinary, something almost familiar about him.

Sunlight angled down and caught the right side of his face, caught the long gray hair parted in the middle and brushed back along the top and sides. The sea wind came and blew his hair, and he reached to push it back from his face, pulled an orange suspender higher on his shoulder, adjusted the leather Swiss Army knife case on his belt. The sun passed behind a cloud, and he fell into shadow for a few seconds before sunlight again came on him.

She experienced an involuntary shudder and had a powerful urge to walk outside and talk with the man. But at that moment, her customer made a decision, holding out a small wood carving and pointing to one of Heather Michaels' photographs on the wall. Working the cash register, Wynn continued glancing toward the window where the man seemed to be staring in at her. The woman making the purchases noticed her behavior and turned to look at the window.

"Do you know that man outside?" she asked,

giving the general impression that she was not receiving Wynn McMillan's full attention.

"Oh, sorry, I...I thought I did for a moment, but I don't think so."

"Rather a peculiar sort of fellow, isn't he." Her well-dressed customer, with whom she had dealt many times before, tended to affect a British manner of living and speaking.

"Yes, he is that, all right. But then, you know Mendocino. All sorts of strange people come and go through here." Wynn began wrapping the artwork. When she looked again toward the window, the man had disappeared.

After returning to the Chevron station, Robert Kincaid paused with his fingers on Harry's door handle and almost went back to the gallery. He always had been clumsy around women he didn't know, embarrassed by his own presence when they spoke to him. He ran the whens and the wheres into his thoughts again, shook his head as if to clear it, and started the engine.

After the shop closed at six, Wynn McMillan went home, still shaken by the image of the man who had looked through the shop window at her. She went out and walked the streets of Mendocino for two hours, hoping to catch a glimpse of him. Finding nothing, she returned by way of the headlands, letting the darkness come over her, listening to the sound of her own footsteps above the slap of waves at low tide and night wind through the cypress. Remembering a far-back time when the sea beat upon the coast of Big Sur and she played Schubert for a man just returned from the wars.

Fifty miles farther down the coast, Robert Kincaid stared straight ahead and listened to the hum of his rubber tires on a road that eventually would lead to Big Sur, if he followed it into morning. He was thinking about the crosshatch of lives and places and events, recollections plotted in three-space. And from that space, sections sliced by time, like a knife through an orange. This particular knife being several decades old and dulled, but still keen enough that he glanced in his rearview mirror and considered Mendocino. The wheres and whens had formed a vague hypothesis. Coincidence, yes. Perhaps. But if coincidence were put aside as implausible, then what to make of most of life, let alone existence itself? The elegance of whimsy is everywhere, and the fact we live at all is implausible, he thought. And somewhere, in the workshops of Who or What with the master hand, chance and grand design are inseparable, a place where the improbable becomes likely and surprise is the rule.

That night, after two places had refused to allow the presence of Highway, Robert Kincaid lay in a small hotel in Sonoma, in darkness, and again considered Mendocino. And he thought of those times when he was young and tanned and iron-hard from his days on the beaches of Tarawa. Having escaped or been released, depending on perspective, he had ridden the curves of Big Sur with a woman behind him, her hair tangled with the wind and streaming back like an older man now reaching for what he wanted to recall and nearly could. Maybe could recall it, if he forced himself to think long and honestly.

And before sleep came that evening, Robert Kincaid's final thoughts were two: denying coincidence while almost hoping for it, coupled with a simultaneous wish to be young again and yet to die within the hour.

8

Big Sur, 1945

Wynn McMillan, toting cello and suitcase, rode into Big Sur on the mail truck. Together with a graceful spirit acquired early on from inheritance more than life, she was fast coming into a similar grace of form and conduct. Those qualities amended what at base level was a certain angular plainness in her physical appearance. As such, with her willowy figure and long brown hair, most would have seen Wynn McMillan as comely.

In her nineteenth year and lacking specific intents other than to play music and live what she saw as the romantic life, Wynn enjoyed a sanguinity flowing from being young and knowing the world was getting better. Germany had surrendered to the Allies three days earlier, and America was in a state of mass euphoria approaching ecstasy. From a long and high view, the end of the fighting could be seen. But across the Pacific, on Okinawa, Buckner's Tenth Army was still driving south against heavy Japanese resistance. Three hundred miles above the Tenth lay the Japanese home ground, the island of Kyushu scheduled for a November assault.

Jake the mailman steered his truck around hairpin curves where dynamite had sculpted a road from what had been mountain, the face of the Santa Lucia Range hard to the left and a four-hundred-foot drop to the ocean only two yards away, on the right. At times, the hood ornament seemed to point toward nothing but infinity, and over it Wynn McMillan could see the cliffs of Big Sur jutting into the Pacific, marching away to the south like the folds of a dark, heavy curtain.

Below them, fog lay in the canyons, and the sea was wrinkled with a row of the eight thousand waves a day that struck the shoreline. When Jake followed the road down into a stretch of meadowland and through the Big Sur Valley, Wynn could see poppies and wild lilacs in bloom. The future could not have seemed more promising to her.

She was freshly washed for this journey into a new stage of her life. Across the Pacific and a few latitudes below Big Sur, Robert Kincaid had not taken a real bath for weeks, and his battle dress clung to him like moldering flesh. Though he was not aware of it, three of his photographs had appeared on major magazine covers in the last two months. The only credit line accompanying the pictures had been "U. S. Marine Photo."

Riding along with Jake, Wynn McMillan had a copy of *Life* stuffed into a side pocket of her large purse. On the cover was a shot of a Marine hosing out a bunker with a flame thrower while other GI's were coming up the hill behind him. Kincaid had made the photo ten days earlier. The Marine with the flame thrower had died when he stepped on a land mine three hours after Kincaid shot the photo.*

---

*Author's note. Seven of Kincaid's Pacific theater photographs subsequently were published in a collection titled *The Visual*

The floppy felt hat resting on Wynn's long brown hair seemed a bit heavy in comparison to the light spring dress she wore. Still, she had wanted to wear the dress and take the hat and so had made a compromise, ignoring the clash of textures.

Wynn McMillan's father, a respected haberdasher in Monterey, would not have approved of her clothing choices, but then he approved of almost nothing his daughter had done through the past few years of her life. The cello was an exception, and he loved to have her play for him in the evenings when supper was finished and her mother, Irene, who had been a theater pianist for silent films, was putting away the dishes. He would sit in his easy chair, in bow tie, crisp shirt, and sharply pressed flannels, and smile and close his eyes and move his head in time with the music. He was especially proud on Easter Sunday each year, when his daughter's quartet played for morning service at the Presbyterian church. As Wynn's cello soared

Art of War. Credit for the work was given to another photographer who acquired the negatives from the Marine Corps and claimed to have done the work. Evidently, Kincaid was not aware of this or, perhaps, as was his nature, he simply shrugged and assumed such dishonesty would gather its own punishments. Five years later, a scholar working in the history of photography discovered the chicanery and published a brief article correcting the error, though twelve thousand copies of the original book remain in various libraries and private hands, with the error perpetuated. The man who plagiarized Kincaid's work became a well-known photographer for a major newspaper and claimed a publishing mixup was responsible for the misrepresentation, though he never apologized to Kincaid and continued to cite the book on his resume, claiming all the photos therein were his own work.

in E major, Malcolm McMillan would turn and smile and nod at those who smiled and nodded back at him.

Beyond the cello, however, Wynn's behavior was a puzzlement to him. Very much in the manner of Robert Kincaid, formal education had never much interested her, and she feigned illness many times to avoid trundling off to another day of what she saw as boring schoolwork. Wynn spent those days playing her cello and reading and teaching herself to paint in oils. In spite of her apparent illnesses during the week, on Saturdays and Sundays she worked long hours helping the Red Cross pack medical supplies for the European front.

In her teens, she began wearing what her father thought were rather quirky getups, a mishmash of scarves and blouses and, lord help him, men's slacks on her long, slim (some would have said bony) frame. Of the young men who called for her occasionally, none seemed conventional enough to satisfy him.

"Irene, doesn't our daughter know any nice young men with good prospects?"

"She is her own young woman, Malcolm. I think she inherited the mutinous nature of all those Scots you're always praising. I've spoken with her a number of times about such matters, and all she does is laugh and say, 'Oh, mother, really. I'm in no hurry to get married. There's a whole world of music and art out there I want to explore. Daddy would have me take up with a doctor or lawyer, settle down and have babies, be playing lullabies on the cello by the time I'm twenty.'"

So Malcolm McMillan, suffering with his wife the memories of their son who had been killed at the taking of Salerno two years earlier, could only shake his head in disappointment when Wynn announced she was going to some place called Big Sur to study composition with the pianist Gerhart Clowser. All Malcolm knew about Big Sur was its association with freethinkers and nonconformists. A subsequent hoax perpetrated by some of the Big Sur residents, playing to the panting need for sensationalism by the press and its readers, would only add to his misery when he read that Big Sur was the home of a cult promoting sex and anarchy.

Wynn's letters did not help Malcolm McMillan's state of mind.

I'm living in a one-room shack built from dynamite boxes discarded in the building of Highway One. No refrigerator, no electric lights, and the toilet is outdoors. Jake, the mailman, hauls kerosene, coal, eggs, and all sorts of things when he brings the mail down from Monterey.

The people here are absolutely fascinating. Zen Buddhists, an expert in Irish folklore, and others who seem to know immense amounts about art, archaeology, linguistics, and on and on. Almost everyone does art, from sculpture to poetry to woodworking. But it's not what most people think: Those who live here on a permanent basis must struggle every day with simply meeting their basic needs. There are plenty of what Daddy would call "characters," but the fakes are mostly those who come down here claiming to be artists, but who never do any art and do not remain here very long. One of those pretenders took the hairpin curve at Hurricane Point too fast last week and went over the cliff. You can see the wreckage of the auto on the rocks below. We all made a field trip up there just to look at the mess. Never found the body.

I'm learning a great deal about composition and music in general from Mr. Clowser, who, by the way, was famous in Europe for his concerts. Guess where I found him? Playing on an upright outside of Emil White's cabin near the highway. He says it's the only piano available to him.

I have to go help some people cut firewood, then we're going down to Slate's hot springs where every-body takes off their clothes and jumps in.

Having a wonderful time and making a little money doing odd jobs and giving cello lessons to a young lady and an eighty-year-old poet. And guess who lives in a cabin on Partington Ridge. None other than Henry Miller. I haven't met him yet, but hope to soon.

Love,
Wynn

"Who is Henry Miller?" Malcolm McMillan asked of his wife.

"He's a writer."

"What sort of things does he write?"

"Malcolm, I don't think you really want to know."

"Yes, I do."

"He wrote, among other things, *Tropic of Cancer.* But you can't buy it in the United States."

"Why not?"

"It's banned as being obscene."

"Obscene? In what way?"

"Malcolm, as I said before, I don't think you really want to know."

~

Four months after Wynn McMillan arrived in Big Sur, came then a lone rider following the same road south she had taken, past Yankee Point and down the Sur Hill Thrust. If one had been standing on the volcanic heights at Point Sur, near the lighthouse and looking inland across clumps of silver lupine, the rider would have been visible only as a dark speck against the Santa Lucia cliffs or as a silhouette when he crossed the high bridges. Perhaps a bright reflection would have glinted now and then from the chromed parts of his Ariel Four motorcycle.

From its inception in 1929, the Ariel Four was a remarkable machine if you were more interested in engine performance than overall mechanical design. Robert Kincaid was no connoisseur of motorcycles; he simply liked the way it looked and felt. After the years of war, of not being able to move without caution and fear, of living close with thousands of other men in ships and bunkers, the Ariel had sat before him in a San Francisco showroom like an instrument of freedom.

"This is a rare one, bought her off an Englishman on his way home to defend his country," the salesman had said. "Take'er down south, along those curves and cliffs, that'll give you a good chance to get the feel of her. Watch'er, though. You turn that twistgrip and she'll be at seventy before you know it."

Big Sur lay in its golden time between the fogs of summer and the winter rains, the sycamores and maples and black oaks were in full color as Robert Kincaid rode across the high bridge over Bixby Creek. Neatly tied behind him, unlike his memories of the war he had just exited, were his sleeping bag, a small clothes duffle, and the rest of his kit.

Farther down the coast he glided to a stop when he saw an elderly man and a young woman engaged in a piano-cello duet outside of a cabin. He shut down the engine and listened. The rustle of black oak leaves fused with the music, and the sensations flooding his brain made him almost dizzy. Somewhere, not long ago, there had been mortars and screams and the clanking of tank gears, and now there was music and the flutter of colored leaves. The old man shook his gray hair as he bent over the keyboard, while the young woman straddled her cello, attentive to the pianist who occasionally lifted his right hand and conducted the music.

Once the pianist stopped completely and spoke to the woman, gesturing, "Allegro, Miss McMillan, yes, but the Rachmaninov is not a horse race, not presto, and with a much lighter touch, please. We'll take it from bar forty-two." First counting time, he began to play again, the woman joining him. At thirty-two, tired from the killing, Robert Kincaid leaned against the Ariel and listened.

After a while, several other people came to sit on the grass and listen to the music. They were dressed simply, the men looking more like woodsmen than the wild-eyed artists who supposedly lived in Big Sur. When the music lesson ended, they came over and introduced themselves, open and friendly. The cellist packed her instrument in a canvas bag and joined them.

One of the men said, "The high cirrus clouds this time of year give us beautiful sunsets. We're going to the beach to watch. Please come along if you like. Harvey over there is going to beach-cook fresh trout from the river, and I can guarantee it will be wonderful. He even cooked a penguin killed on the highway once, and I'm here to tell you it was delicious."

And in the night, as they ate Harvey's trout and talked long afterward and listened to a man named Hugh play an Irish harp, the waves pounding on the sea stacks sounded like the roll of distant battleship guns. To Robert Kincaid, not long removed from blood and slaughter, this was an otherworld, real and unreal at the same time. He would lurch from the calm of easy laughter, from the voices talking philosophy and art and music, to a jolting sense of where he had been and what he had seen. His skin was copper and his eyes were old, and when someone asked about his life, he said only that he had been traveling.

The cellist, whose name was Wynn, noticed he said little and came to sit beside him, to draw him out of his silence. She introduced herself and shook his hand. He told her his name, but as with all such gatherings, names of strangers do not sharply register and lock down in permanent memory.

After talking to him for twenty minutes, she asked, "What is your first name, again?"

"Robert," he said. "And yours is...Wynn, did you say?"

"Yes. Scottish name." She spelled it for him. "My father is very proud of his heritage."

She stared at Robert Kincaid through the flicker of a beach fire and noticed what everyone first noticed about him: his eyes. Eyes that gave the appearance of looking through and beyond whatever was at hand. In those eyes, and also in his movements, was a quality that simultaneously was fearsome and loving, something of the warrior and a hint of the poet, as if he were one together with some other time far back and ever gone. She had the feeling that if she put a mirror to his face, something strange and primitive might be reflected.

"What do you do? For a living, I mean? I heard you say earlier you've been traveling."

"I've been in the South Pacific, in the Marines. Just got out a little while ago. I was a photographer before the War, and that's what I'll try to do again."

"What was your job in the Marines?"

"Same thing, photography."

Robert Kincaid stared at the sand and found it astonishing that he was sitting quietly there, instead of dragging his six-feet-two-inches along it, under sputtering sheets of machine-gun fire. For a moment, he was back on the atolls, leaning over his assistant, calling for a medic. Then a woman's voice was talking to him again.

"I sometimes come here to practice my cello in the afternoons. If you'd like to join me tomorrow, we could make a picnic of it."

The fire was burning low, people were leaving, going to their homes on the ridges or in the canyons.

A voice to his right was saying, "It'll be all right. Jake's bringing kerosene on Wednesday. I ordered enough for several months, so I can let you have some."

People shook Kincaid's hand, said they had enjoyed meeting him, and walked into the night. A man named Lawrence came over and said Kincaid was welcome to bed down at his place, an offer accepted with thanks.

Waves pounded at the sea stacks, the sound of them, as before, like the long guns on American warships. On Betio, a medic had bent over Kincaid's assistant and said, "Sorry, he's gone, dead before he hit the ground. Goddamned snipers, anyway," as he ripped off the dog tags from the boy-man who had been learning photography from Kincaid. "Keep your head down, the snipers are out there on that hulk of a Jap merchantman."

"Well," the young woman's voice said. "Picnic or not?"

"Oh, yes. Uh…it sounds…sounds great. I'd love to do it."

"Good. I'll meet you at the turnoff from the highway at, say, two tomorrow afternoon. Day after tomorrow, we're going to visit Henry Miller.

You're welcome to join us."

Kincaid knew of Henry Miller. Though his books were banned in the United States, they had been a familiar commodity among the soldiers overseas.

"That might be interesting. He's not necessarily my cup of tea, but it should be—well, as I said—interesting."

"Oh, Henry's pretty harmless in his current state. He wanders around here like everyone else and tries to avoid all the gullible people who make pilgrimages to see him, people expecting nothing but naked bodies lying all over in various states of indecent behavior."

≈

Malcolm McMillan still saw his daughter as she had been at fifteen, a little gawky and with what he always thought was not enough meat on her bones.

"That girl needs to eat more," he would mention to his wife.

"Malcolm, you haven't been paying attention. In the last two years she's started to fill out her clothing in a rather womanly manner. The way she dresses pretty well conceals that most of the time. And she's lost her awkwardness, has become rather graceful, I'd say."

Even through the baggy slacks and light sweater she wore, Robert Kincaid did notice the shape and curve of Wynn McMillan's figure as he slowed the Ariel and came to a stop where she stood by the highway. Only recently had a tinge of the old eagerness returned. In a state of continence enforced by the circumstances of war on remote islands, he had focused on staying alive and doing his job. Under those conditions, except for the nurses who were as tired and worn as the infantry, women had been abstractions: the Rita Hayworth pinup in the cramped quarters of a troopship, the folded picture of Lauren Bacall a Marine carried in his breast pocket, the photos of wives and girl friends passed around for others to admire and share in the loneliness. And, of course, the velvet, coaxing radio voice of several different women generically called "Tokyo Rose," urging the GI's to desert in the face of a hopeless cause.

But the sun was warm and the afternoon lay before Robert Kincaid like another lifetime, a prize awarded by Providence and little else as he saw it, thinking himself no more or less deserving than those who had fallen even as he photographed them. Sixteen million Americans had been mobilized for the War, four hundred thousand had died in battle or from related events. The Japanese had lost two million.

"Hello," she said as he swung his leg off the Ariel. She was smiling, and Kincaid thought she looked quite beautiful.

"Hello. Great day, huh?" he said, suddenly realizing it was now a time for smiling. The act of smiling and the laughter of the sane were skills he was trying to learn all over again.

"It's hardly ever not beautiful in Big Sur. Stay around and you'll see that." She tilted her head in a manner underscoring the invitation.

Kincaid kept on smiling and patted the Ariel's

seat, glancing at her cello and the wicker basket sitting beside her. "Looks as if we might require a logistics officer, something like coming ashore at Guadalcanal, though that turned out to be a mess. Since I need both hands to operate the bike, I'll strap your basket and my knapsack on the back. If you can manage to sling the cello over your shoulder by the case strap, you can climb on behind me, and I'll take it real easy and try to stop the whole business before we hit the water."

The land was canopied by sycamores and sloped downward to the beach, sunlight working through the leaves and freckling the shadowed road. Kincaid parked the Ariel against a cliff face thirty yards from the Pacific, well above what he judged was the high-tide line.

Wynn McMillan pointed north. "We could walk along the shore, go around that headland over there to a lovely small beach sheltered from the wind. We need to watch the tide, however. It's low presently, but when it comes back in there's no way around the headland except to climb the cliffs or wait for low tide again."

Military canteen hanging from one side of his belt, Swiss Army knife affixed to the other side, Robert Kincaid slung the cello over his right shoulder and hoisted the knapsack over his left shoulder. She carried the wicker basket with ham sandwiches, potato salad, and two bottles of red wine. She originally packed only one bottle, but thinking of how the man had looked in the firelight the previous evening, she decided a second bottle might be in order. One never knew.

She talked of music and the sea and her growing
love for Big Sur, and he noticed the way she used
her hands, the movements being quick arabesques,
almost musical. He watched as she hunted shells
and thought it had been a long time since he paid
attention to seashells aside from the nasty cuts they
provided when you fell on them or crawled over
them on your way up the beaches.

She looked over her shoulder at him, smiled
warmly, then turned and asked, "Why do you wear
both a belt and those wide suspenders? Is it an indi-
cation of some inner anxiety?"

Kincaid laughed. "I don't, always. Depends on
what I'm doing. By the time I hang a canteen, a
light meter, the knife, and a few other things on my
belt, my pants start to slide down. So I use suspenders to counter that tendency."

After a half-hour walk across hard-packed sand,
Kincaid savoring the young woman's curiosity and
enthusiasm for all that surrounded her, enjoying
the swing of her hips as she walked before him, they
rounded the headland.

He would later write this:

*We came to a small beach in mid-afternoon, took
off our shoes, and forded a shallow mountain creek
cutting its way across the sand to the Pacific. The
creek was an odd bluish-purple color, which I would
later find was caused by its run over volcanic rock
on the way to the sea. Watching the waves beat upon
the shore rocks, I almost overlooked an unusual
track in the sand at my feet. The print was about
three feet wide and smooth, with gouges on either*

side of it at even intervals.

Squatting, I touched the marks, as if they might speak of what created them. Except for the breakers and the sound of my own breathing, there was silence. I let my eyes follow the track toward the water. Something large and brown was at the end of that strange path. Something large and brown and moving. I glanced at the woman. She too had seen whatever it was.

I had only a small rangefinder camera in my knapsack and dug for it as I moved forward. Carefully I went. This was not my territory, and I was unfamiliar with the wildlife of both the forest and the sea, and the sheer size of this animal was intimidating. Circling, I tried to get ahead of whatever was there on the sand, only thirty yards distant.

I could see the face, mounted on a body fifteen feet in length and weighing several thousand pounds. It was a strange, sad face, with brown eyes resembling smooth beach stones and with a trunklike proboscis. Using its flippers, the animal heaved its way along the sand toward the water. It saw me and raised its head for a better view, then lowered it again and lay upon the sand in the way a dog lies upon a carpet, chin down, watching me, blinking.

From twenty feet, the brown eyes showed clearly in the lens. They were looking directly at me, a look of fear or at least a wary inquisitiveness as I crouched and tried to find a good angle. I began to sort through the feelings I've always had about disrupting the lives of other living things with my intrusions, and, clearly, the woman and I had intruded upon a peaceful moment that could have done without us.

I flogged my memory for the images in all the wildlife manuals I had read over the years. I should have known the creature, but didn't, couldn't remember. Not a sea lion. Wrong nose, too big. Not a walrus, yet in size and behavior it had that look. Though I have never been passionate about remembering the names of things, and, in fact, always have believed we are too intent on labeling the world about us, I was frustrated at not being able to recall the name of this creature before me.

The animal was placed wrong for a good photograph. Low on the sand, rocks immediately to its rear of the same color as its hide. It didn't matter. I lowered the camera and simply let it be. Then I remembered. The creature was an elephant seal, nearly exterminated by hunters in the nineteenth century and still rarely seen. It had spent the day, perhaps the previous night also, far up the beach and, as all of us eventually seem to do, was struggling toward the water.

Six-foot waves hammered the old rocks as the seal lunged into the shallows, stopping momentarily to look back at the woman and me. The water deepened, and the animal's awkwardness began to disappear. On land it was a huge lump of mud. In the water, something else. Suddenly, sleek and fast, sliding deep, disappearing in a moment through a narrow channel between two rocks.

I straightened and looked at the woman. She came over to me, put her arm around my waist. I was still watching the water. She tugged on my shirt sleeve and I looked down at her.

"That was special, Robert," she said. "They are

*not often seen around here." She smiled and looked
straight at me.*

*After a moment, she added, "Sort of like you, I
think...maybe, not often seen."*

*A three-foot track remained in the sand, with flip-
per marks on either side, leading toward the Pacific.
I put the camera back in the knapsack, thinking yet
about the brown eyes of* Mirounga angustirostris *as it
had studied me, flogging its memory and its manuals, finally recognizing me, and then rolling through
the foam into deep water. Gone.*

*The woman spread a cloth on the ground, near a
rock of a size and height just right for a chair. She took
her cello from the case, tuned it, sat on the rock and
began to play. I lay on the sand and thought of where
I'd been for the last three years, then tried not to think
about it. The sand was warm and I stayed there for a
long time and didn't want to be anywhere else.*

The following morning arrived with heavy fog.
Robert Kincaid scrounged tinder and rekindled
the fire he built the evening before and which
burned through most of the night. He and Wynn
McMillan lay on the sand, holding each other, and
he felt himself becoming young again, shedding
the effects of a war that had made old men out of
new ones.

She was cold, and her long hair had partly fallen
from the comb that had kept it high and neat. Still,
she smiled and kissed him, kissed him again. And
they lay there and touched one another until the
sky turned an oyster color and the sun was a pale
dispersed light through the fog. It was the third

time they had made love since coming to the beach.

"Will you stay on, then?" she asked later.

He sat up and brushed sand from his palms, pulled on his boots and began to lace them. "I can't. I need work and have to call *National Geographic* to see if they have anything for me. I did a lot of assignments for them prior to the War. I'm thinking of locating in the San Francisco area. It's not far. We can see each other often."

"I know. But I sometimes wish life was like this all the time, like last night, like this morning." She leaned against Kincaid's damp shirt and fiddled with his collar.

His head was canted against the top of hers, and he could smell the sea in her hair. Out of the fog, a flock of brown pelicans came, beating their way south in an irregular line only inches above the water. They disappeared into the mist and were replaced by gulls beginning their morning's work. As good as that moment was, Robert Kincaid knew it could not be suspended in aspic, carried forward unchanged. And there was a certain restlessness within him. A second lifetime stretched before him, and he was impatient to get on with it.

Wynn McMillan unfastened the top two buttons of his shirt, kissed his chest, leaving her face against his skin for some moments while Robert Kincaid stroked her hair and felt grains of sand sprinkled through it. She turned her head and rested against him, pointing toward the ocean, whispering, "The gray whales come by in March, they say."

9

Autumn 1981

Thirty-six years and three months beyond the autumn beaches of Big Sur, November in South Dakota lingered hard and graceless, a telling prelude to what lay waiting in the form of serious winter. Already, much of what flew or ran had headed south or gone to ground. Carlisle McMillan noticed people's attitudes had changed, the faces pinched in resignation, readying themselves for months of indoor living. Even their postures seem to have become stooped, as if they had grown a carapace and pulled in their heads, holding their breaths until the thaws of March and April.

The library in Falls City was over-warm, radiators at the final stage of an archaic coal-fired heating system clanking and hissing. The building was nearly empty in midmorning, the only sounds apart from the heating system being those of a crackling newspaper as an elderly woman turned its pages, along with the almost noiseless work of a librarian replacing books on shelves. Twice the librarian had looked in Carlisle's direction, wondering if an Indian had come in from Rosebud or Wounded Knee.

Carlisle checked *Who's Who* for the name of one Robert L. Kincaid and found nothing. The librarian working the reference desk consulted his directory of directories and informed Carlisle that a separate guide, similar to *Who's Who*, existed specifically for those in the photography profession.

"It should be in the second row of shelves in the reference section, I believe, close to where you found *Who's Who*."

Sitting at a well-polished table of honest construction and of a vintage appealing to him, Carlisle ran his fingers over the white oak and stared at the book before him. He opened it to the "K" section and let his eyes move slowly down the columns.

Kincaid, Robert L. b. August 1, 1913, Barnesville, OH; f. Thomas H., m. Agnes. w. Marian Waterson, 1953, div. 1957. U.S. Army 1931–35; USMC 1943–45. Notable awards: "Distinguished Achievement," American Society of Photographers; "Lifetime of Excellence," *International Journal of Photography*. Free-lancer, primarily for *National Geographic*. Other assignments for *Life, Time, Globetrotter*, similar major magazines. Photojournalist specializing in exotic, sometimes dangerous, locations. Known for poetic renderings of subjects mundane and otherwise. Address: unknown.

Robert Kincaid, whoever he was, would be sixty-eight, Carlisle thought, studying what there was of the information. He went into the library stacks, found the bound volumes of *National Geographic*, and carried an armload, dating from 1978 forward, to another table. It took him nearly an hour to leaf through the pages, scanning two articles of general interest to him along the way. But there was nothing about anyone named Robert Kincaid.

He began a methodical search, working backward through the issues, year by year. In the February 1975 issue was an article on wheat combining in the Great Plains featuring Kincaid's photography. He found other pieces in 1974 and 1973. A footnote to a 1972 article on Acadia National Park indicated Kincaid had broken an ankle during the shoot. Not only did Carlisle admire the photography of this Kincaid, he also appreciated the old boy's perseverance and stamina. At fifty-nine, Kincaid had still been out there with his cameras, walking the cliffs.

After lunch at a cafe on the city square, Carlisle returned to the library and continued his search. As he moved back through the years, more and more of Kincaid's work appeared in the magazine. Finally, related to a 1967 article on the disappearing jungles of East Africa, Carlisle McMillan found what he wanted: a photograph of the man, on the back page of the magazine. Robert Kincaid was squatting down by an African river, obviously studying something in front of him, camera held at chest level. His long hair drifted well over his shirt collar, and he wore a silver chain around his neck, with some sort of medallion attached to the chain.

And it was then Carlisle shuddered and leaned back against the chair for a moment, staring at the high ceiling of the Carnegie building. The man in the photograph was wearing wide, orange suspenders. Wynn had remembered the suspenders.

A large group of school children was coming into the library, chattering and sliding on the floor in spite of a teacher's best efforts to restrain them. Carlisle sat for the next few minutes, staring at the photograph of a man hunkered down in East Africa, a man who held a camera and wore suspenders. He marked the page with a slip of library reference paper and began working further back into the volumes.

All told, he found twenty-eight articles, some dating to the late 1930s, for which Robert Kincaid had done the photography. In six of the articles, the text was also credited to him. There were four distinct photographs of Kincaid, one from a 1948 issue. The long hair had not yet turned gray at that time and, though Carlisle realized it could have been his imagination, the hair seemed to be exactly the same shade of brown as his own. The nose and cheekbones were similar, too, with almost American Indian features. Carlisle, however, clearly was larger in body than Kincaid, a product of his wild, warrior heritage of Scottish clansmen, as his mother liked to say.

Carlisle photocopied every page of every article in which Robert Kincaid had participated, plus the four pictures of him. His intent was to survey other major magazines from the thirties forward, but the library was closing early that day for a staff meeting. He finished the photocopying and went back to his truck. Driving the forty miles to his house northwest of Salamander, Carlisle became aware of how much his search had focused on Robert Kincaid to the exclusion of other possibilities. There were other "Roberts," surely, but for some reason Kincaid seemed to have a hammerlock on Carlisle's mind, and he had neglected to notice if any other photographers of that given name had articles in *National Geographic*.

Looking down his headlights into the November darkness, he wondered about that, about what tapping way back and far down might be causing him to concentrate on this elusive man named Kincaid. He convinced himself it was because of the close fit between what Wynn said about the man she had known in Big Sur plus Buddy's report on the motorcycle.

That evening, Carlisle spread the photocopies on the floor and sorted them according to location. Most were in distant places such as India, Africa, Guatemala, Spain, Australia. Two were in Canada. In the United States, one was in Iowa, another in the Louisiana bayous, one in Maine, and two more in the Far West.

Dumptruck roused from his place under the wood stove and came to lie purring on a stack of photocopies.

"Suppertime, Big Guy? Sorry, I've been neglecting you."

While Dumptruck worked on a can of tuna, Carlisle held one of the photocopies directly under the kitchen light and studied it. The reproduction was crisp, and the man named Robert Kincaid looked out at him from the picture. He put it down, picked it up again, staring hard. Jesus, he had missed something, and there it was: the bracelet on the man's right wrist. Wynn had mentioned a bracelet. Suspenders, bracelet, an "A" on the gas tank of the motorcycle, and a Robert L.

Kincaid who had registered the bike in 1945.

Carlisle went back to his desk, studying the diagram he drew earlier and the list of clues he initially wrote down, then sketched a table on a yellow legal pad, trembling a little as he began to check off the clues. When he finished, there was not a blank space opposite his original list.

	Robert L. Kincaid
"A" = Ariel Four Bike	✓
Reg. SF. 9/45	✓
Photographer	✓
Traveled a lot	✓
Free-lance	✓
Magazines	✓
WWII	✓
Marines	✓
Bracelet	✓
Suspenders	✓
"Early 30s" = Age 32 in 1945	✓

"Dumper, it's getting a little scary," he said to the cat sitting on the living room floor, licking itself with long gliding strokes. Carlisle leaned on the windowsill, looking out at the South Dakota darkness.

That night, he lay awake for a long time. Over the easy crackle of the wood stove in the living room, he thought about Robert Kincaid, about the articles he had read. The man in jeans and khaki shirts and suspenders truly had lived an itinerant life, a nomad across the face of the Earth. If he was the man of Wynn's memory, no wonder they had lost track of one another. His mother had moved around a fair amount in her younger years, and Kincaid apparently had never been in any one place for long. He called up the eyes of Robert Kincaid in his mind, and the man looked back at him from somewhere in East Africa.

~

Two days after his research at the Falls City Library, Carlisle McMillan placed a call to the Washington, D.C., offices of *National Geographic*. He had forgotten about the one-hour time difference, and a secretary said everyone had gone to lunch, but perhaps she could help in some way. "Just who is it, again, you're looking for?"

"His name is Robert Kincaid. According to a number of articles I have, he did a lot of work for the magazine from the 1930s to 1975. I'm trying to locate him. There's a chance he might be a relative."

"Yes, everybody seems to be doing genealogy these days. My husband is tracing his family tree. This will take a minute. Can you hold?"

"Sure, I'll hold on." Carlisle tapped a pencil on a notepad and waited. Dumptruck jumped on Carlisle's lap and swatted at the pencil. Carlisle moved the pencil rapidly back and forth along the table edge, the cat's head intently following the movements between swats at it. Outside, the sky was low and somber, drops of icy rain hitting the windows.

The secretary came back on the line. "Sorry to take so long. I had to dig into the inactive files. If we're talking about the same Robert Kincaid, you're correct. He did a lot of work for the magazine over a period of years. Our records show his last assignment was in 1975. Apparently, he was quite a rambler. Somebody wrote at the top of his file, 'Will go anywhere and stay as long as it takes to get the job done. Can be trusted to bring home the bacon.'"

"Do your records say anything about him being in the military in World War II?" Carlisle asked. He could hear the rustle of turning pages on the other end.

"Yes, he was in the Marines. There's an old resume here; says he was discharged in September of 1945 at age thirty-two. That was his second tour of duty. He was in the Army earlier, finished his hitch in '35, went to work for us, then the military apparently wanted him back again when World War II started, but he joined the Marines that time. He was born in Barnesville, Ohio, and graduated from high school there. That's about all there is, except for a long list of the articles he did for us, which you already seem to know about."

She paused for a moment. "Wait, something just occurred to me. I seem to recall pulling this Kincaid's file about a year ago. Someone else was asking about him."

"Do you have any idea who it might have been? Man, woman?"

"Let me see. I think it may have been a woman, but I'm not sure. I had just started work here and transferred the call to one of the associate editors. He asked me to bring him the file. That's all I remember. I'd connect you with that editor, but he's since left the magazine, and I don't know where he is."

"Would you have an address, a phone number for Mr. Kincaid?"

"I show an address in Bellingham, Washington, and a phone number."

Carlisle wrote down the address and number, thanked the woman for her help, and hung up. He thought about it for a moment, then dialed the phone number in Bellingham, not quite sure what he would say if Robert Kincaid answered. He need not have worried about it. An agent for an insurance company answered and told him the company had been assigned the number two years before when the new branch office opened. Sorry about that. But was Carlisle interested, perhaps, in talking about the innovative annuity program they were offering? Carlisle was not interested.

He next tried the Bellingham Chamber of Commerce. According to the city directory, no Robert Kincaid lived in Bellingham. The address he had been given was now a shopping center, which had been constructed in 1979. Carlisle was frustrated, momentarily depressed almost, feeling as if he were looking down the wrong end of a telescope. He had seemed to be getting close, but now felt otherwise. The man named Robert Kincaid could be anywhere, or buried deep in the earth, for that matter.

He was almost at the point of giving up the whole project. Reaching back too many years encompassing too many dead ends, he was tracking an elusive shadow with a half-penny's evidence. About the only way he could be part-sure of anything would be to find this Kincaid and ask him if he made love to a woman on a Big Sur beach in the autumn of 1945. And that still wouldn't prove anything, conclusively, even if it were so. If things were as free and easy in Big Sur as Wynn remembered, maybe there was another man with whom she was involved around that time. He hadn't considered that possibility and wasn't quite sure how he would go about asking his mother.

In late afternoon, after splitting wood for two hours and showering, Carlisle stood on his front porch and looked out across the countryside, toward Wolf Butte shrouded in mist. He went inside and sat by the stove, reading again the articles he photocopied at the Falls City Library, searching for a clue, a lead, anything he had overlooked.

~

Eight miles from where Carlisle McMillan sat by his wood stove, an aging green pickup, with "Kincaid Photography, Bellingham, Washington" in faded and almost invisible letters painted on both doors, came down the evening main street of Salamander, South Dakota. Robert Kincaid parked the truck and went into a tavern called Leroy's. Three men in Stetsons and cowboy boots were at the bar laughing, but quieted and looked at the newcomer with something less than friendly eyes.

Leroy came along behind the bar and asked what the stranger wanted to drink.

Robert Kincaid said nothing right at the moment, thanks, and inquired about the man who had been his guide some years ago when Kincaid had done a shoot on an archeological dig west of town.

"Yeah, he lives across the street, above what used to be Lester's TV and Appliance. Still as cantankerous as ever, too."

On second thought, Kincaid bought a six-pack of beer from Leroy and walked across the street. There was a light on in the room above Lester's. Kincaid climbed the stairs and knocked, reaching down to massage his bad ankle while he waited.

"Who the hell is it and whaddya want?" came an old scratchy voice from inside.

Kincaid said who he was, and the door swung open.

"By god, the hippie photographer from out west!" He clapped Kincaid on the shoulder. "I know you ain't no hippie, but your damn ol' long hair always makes me think of them nothing-to-do-but-screw-around bastards. Come on in and be sure and bring that beer in your hand along with you. Been…how long since you were here doing all that photography?"

Kincaid told him it had been eight years and asked if he might bring Highway up rather than leaving him in the pickup.

"Hell, yes," the old man said. "Ain't met him yet, but like dogs, overall. Hardly ever met a dog without all the elements of good character—trust, loyalty, honor, all that. Can't say the same for most people I've met."

With his outlook, the old guy could run a motel in Astoria, Oregon, Kincaid thought, as he led Highway up the creaky stairs lighted by only a single bulb at the top.

So the night went. They talked of life and the road, about the War years when the questions of right and wrong were clear for all to see, and liberties juggled like delicate crystal in the hands of those far too young for the tossing. They talked of the old fellow's great love for a French girl from his World War II days following the liberation of Paris.

Kincaid asked after the accordion man who sometimes played at Leroy's.

"Yeah, Gabe's still playing there. Saturday nights only, so you're a little early. If you can stick around till Saturday, we can go over and get drunk and shout down the yahoos when they complain about Gabe playing too many tangos and not enough cowboy shit. By chance, Gabe was in Paris same time as I was and learned the tangos from musicians in those little cafes. Got real taken by that music. Always makes me a little misty when I hear those songs coming from across the street on Saturday nights. Makes me think about Paris…and Amélie."

Kincaid said he would like to stay, but had to move on the next morning.

"Well, in that case, you can flop down on my sofa if you want, spend the night. Gimme one of them cigarettes I see bulgin' in your shirt pocket. I ran out two days ago, and this damn leg of mine that got mangled by a front-end loader, a year or two after you came by in '73, has been actin' up, so I ain't left the apartment for all these two-days' time."

Kincaid took Highway for an evening stroll, letting him do what Highway did. Rain with bits of ice mixed in with it had begun to fall, and the main street of Salamander was deserted except for a few vehicles parked in front of Leroy's. Stopping by the pickup, Kincaid took out his sleeping bag before climbing the stairs again to the old man's apartment. Halfway up, a sharp pain hit him in the chest, and he leaned against the wall, at once feeling short of breath and slightly nauseous, as if his entire system were threatening to shut down. The feeling passed after a minute or two, and he finished the climb, wondering about himself.

Before they turned in for the night, the old man said, "Ever get wind of that strange crap that went on out at the archeological dig after you took the pictures of it?"

Kincaid shook his head.

"Started up no more'n a month or two after you left. There'd been rumors for some time about all sorts of weird goings-on, lights flashing from up on Wolf Butte, people claiming some giant bird was circling the excavation at night. Like I said, all sorts of crazy stuff. The main man on the dig fell off a butte and smashed himself to death. All the other people working out there packed up and pulled out not long after that."

Kincaid thought for a moment before replying. "That is strange stuff. I recall there was talk among the archeologists about an ancient cult dedicated to the worship of some priestess, something to do with the last traces of a civilization that had come across the land bridges from Asia."

"Well, don't matter. Over and done with," sighed the old man. "Young fella moved into old man Williston's place out there not far from Wolf Butte, and he don't seem to be worried. Anyway, I think we're both near to collapsin', so maybe I'll just turn off the lights."

"That sounds good to me," Kincaid said. "I'm beat."

In the darkness a light snow had begun to fall, and in the morning Robert Kincaid spent a few minutes brushing off Harry. On the second floor of a nearby building, the old man leaned from a window and called to him.

"Don't be so long in stopping by next time. Always got a place here for you to stay."

Kincaid waved to him, backed Harry into the street, and turned east, toward Iowa.

10

Other Possibilities

Carlisle McMillan called his mother at the Mendocino art gallery.

Her voice was bright. "Carlisle, this is more like it. I've heard more from you in the last few weeks than in the last few years."

"Wynn, I have to ask you something real personal. I wouldn't even think about doing this, but it's critical to the search I'm doing."

Wynn's voice softened, a hint of caution coming into it. "Well, let's hear the question first."

"Was there…I mean…damn, this is hard to ask of a mother…was there any other man with whom you had a relationship in Big Sur?" Carlisle took a deep breath. "What I'm saying, is there any chance I'm looking for the wrong person?"

From Mendocino, there was silence for a moment. "Carlisle, I've never kept much from you, but now you're getting close to being impertinent, you know."

"I know. But, as I said, it's important. I could be on the wrong track, entirely."

"I see what you mean," Wynn McMillan answered, still soft in her voice and obviously thinking.

Carlisle waited, guessing by the silence he was correct.

Finally, Wynn spoke in direct terms. "The answer

is yes. There were two others, and believe me it's something I considered carefully when I discovered I was pregnant. For Mr. X, the dates didn't add up. I would have had to have been pregnant for eleven months for that to have worked out. Mr. Y came along after I was pregnant, but wasn't absolutely sure of it yet. It's…it's more than a little difficult talking about this to my son…to you."

"Wynn…look…I don't make judgments about that sort of thing, even when it involves my mother. I needed the information, that's all, and I'm sorry I had to ask. But there was no other way to find out."

"I understand. Whoops, here comes a customer in the door. Got to go. When we talk again I'll tell you about something peculiar that happened the other day."

"Tell me now, if it's important."

"Just my creativity working overtime, I think."

"Okay. Thanks, Wynn."

"Well, you're welcome, I suppose. Next time, call me and talk about the weather or something like that."

"Okay, bye."

"Bye, Carlisle."

Carlisle sat by the phone and thought for a long time, staring at the face of Robert Kincaid in the photocopies on his desk.

11

Roseman Bridge

Francesca Johnson stood in her living room and watched the rain. Since first light it had come and gone, come again, turning the pastures limp and flattened. Fog rose out of the distant valley where Middle River lay and seemed to be moving steadily toward the house as the day passed. With the outside temperature dropping into the thirties, there was a good chance of snow in early evening, according to WHO radio in Des Moines.

The phone on the kitchen wall rang, sounding far and lonely in the silent house. Francesca caught it on the fourth ring.

"Hi, Mom. Just checking in to see how you're doing," said Carolyn, coming down the line from Burlington, Vermont.

Francesca smiled. The children, still young to her, always sounded grown up from a long way off. Carolyn at thirty-two, Michael a year older, struggling with marriages and lives of their own. Carolyn was in the eighth month of her second pregnancy, and talk about babies dominated the five minutes they spoke with one another.

"Can you come visit when the baby is born?" Carolyn asked. "The timing should be perfect. My classes end ten days before the due date. Then I can take a break and pay attention to Melinda and get the baby launched before starting my thesis."

"I'll try to come. No...what I am saying is, of course I'll be there."

"Good. You've got to get away from the farm once in a while, Mom. Since Dad died I have this image of you sitting there all alone day after day."

"No, I'm really doing very well, Carolyn. Don't worry about me. I have plenty of things to keep me occupied." That was not exactly true, but close enough. "I'm getting a lot of reading done, and I've been teaching as a substitute in Winterset once or twice a month."

"Still trying to ram poetry down their throats?"

"Yes, and still failing." She didn't mention that each time she introduced the students to W. B. Yeats, she thought of Robert Kincaid and his recitation of "Song of Wandering Aengus."

"Is Floyd Clark still trying to get you to go out with him?"

"Yes," Francesca laughed gently. "I think I've put him off enough times that he's starting to get the message."

"Yuk, Floyd Clark. You can do a lot better than that," Carolyn admonished, exhibiting the protectiveness of the child grown and the minor cruelty of the still-young and reasonably attractive.

"Well, maybe. But, nonetheless, it's kind of him to ask me out. I feel a little sorry for Floyd now that Marge is gone, but not sorry enough to accept his offers, I guess." Francesca looked out the kitchen window at stubbled fields, a wet autumn moving rapidly toward a winter that could start before the day was finished.

The talk went on, family talk, before Carolyn

said, "Got to run, Mom. David's coming home from work early so we can attend Lamaze class together. I talked with brother Michael down in Florida, yesterday, and he said to tell you he'll call on your birthday."

"That'll be nice. I always enjoy talking with the two of you and hearing about your busy lives."

"Okay, Mom. Bye, take care. I love you. Talk to you on your birthday."

"I love you, too, Carolyn."

Shortly after three-thirty in the afternoon, Francesca pulled on her rubber chore boots and draped a yellow rain slicker over a sweater and light jacket, tucking her hair inside the hood. She stepped off the porch and began her walk, turning right at the end of the lane, once again heading toward Roseman Bridge.

~

Robert Kincaid avoided passing through Winterset on his way to Roseman Bridge. Aside from the possibility that Francesca Johnson might be in town for the day, the main route from Winterset to the bridge ran directly past her farm. He was not about to turn a sentimental last visit into an act of clumsy self-indulgence, which could be embarrassing to both him and Francesca. That is, if she still lived in Madison County. Who knew, maybe she and her husband had moved to a retirement community in Arizona. He had heard people in the Midwest were inclined to do that.

The bridge lay nine miles or so southwest of the town. He turned south off Route 92 at Greenfield, then worked his way east and north again over a series of secondary roads that were paved for a distance, eventually turning to graveled surfaces as he neared the bridge. With each mile, his breath seemed to be deserting him, and it had nothing to do with angina or whatever evil might be milling around in his primary organs.

He came north over a rise near a small church, and Middle River lay below him, the old bridge standing where it had been for a hundred years. He parked Harry in a grove of trees a hundred yards from the bridge and got out, stashing one camera beneath his lightweight parka and pulling a ball cap low over his eyes.

"Highway, I think I'm going to leave you in the truck. I need to do this thing by myself." The retriever was disappointed and barked twice as he watched Kincaid walk down a gravel road. Kincaid turned, smiled, and went back to the truck.

"Okay, okay, you can come along."

Nose to the ground, the dog ranged ahead of him as they rounded a curve and started down a gently sloping hill toward the bridge.

&

To hold a grievance against fate accomplishes nothing; things occur without reason or rhyme, and no more can be said. Railing against such fortune is to censure wood smoke or wind and to be sorrowed

*through all the days of your passing. In the end, there
is nothing left except to shoulder whatever you have
been handed and to go on.*

Francesca Johnson listened to the spattering of
rain on her slicker hood and remembered reading
those words somewhere, maybe in one of the books
she received from her mail-order book club. And in
her own way, she held no such grievances and was
reasonably content. When she sorrowed, it was not
because she made the decision sixteen years ago to
stay with her family instead of leaving with Robert
Kincaid. The sorrow came from having been
required to make the choice fate and her own
actions had put before her.

After Richard died, she stopped trying to thrust
aside her memories of Robert Kincaid, of their time
together, and simply let him come into her mind
whenever he wanted to. God, he seemed Life itself
to her back then, full of energy and physical power,
talking of the road and dreams and loneliness. And
in the nights of their days with each other, and in
the days as well, she had taken him into her and
loved him with a kind of intensity springing from all
the years of a suppressed and desperate longing for
something she couldn't even articulate until Robert
Kincaid rolled into her life.

Sometimes in her silent bed, with Carolyn's old
phonograph playing "Autumn Leaves," she would
caress her breasts and imagine him there again,
moving over her and taking her like the leopard she
had called him in the journals she kept. Was it only
sixteen years ago? It felt longer. Another lifetime.

Another way of being. And yet on other nights when her mind came around to hold him, it seemed he had been with her only a moment before.

Robert Kincaid was to her, among other things, a gracious man, representing a kind of civility she saw in decline everywhere she looked. He could have tried devious means of reaching her over the years. But he paid attention when she spoke of her family and why she could never leave. And she was sure his silence was only because he did not want to cause her pain by exposing what had happened between the two of them.

She tried to imagine what it would be like if they should ever meet again. Even at her age, would she behave like a school girl on her first date? Would he still be a little awkward and shy, as when they had first met? Would they still want to make love or maybe just sit in her kitchen and remember? She hoped they would make love.

No matter how hard she tried to be truthful with her images, no matter how much she tried honest extrapolation from the way he had been to the way he might be now, she still saw Robert Kincaid as he stepped from his truck, on a summer afternoon. And she always would see him that way, she suspected. As such, she supposed she was the same as anyone else who has loved another person for a long time. Seeing them always in soft focus was a form of kindly protection rather than dishonesty.

And there was part of her that believed he was no longer alive. As months, years, went by, that part seemed to grow in her thoughts, though she could never reconcile herself to that possibility.

Behind her she heard a vehicle coming along the road. Harmon, Floyd Clark's hired man, slowed down to pass her and was careful not to splatter mud. When he was safely past, Harmon accelerated toward the Clark farm three miles farther east. Francesca walked on, her boots making sucking noises where the mud pulled at them. She was a mile from Roseman Bridge.

~

Robert Kincaid scouted the bridge from a distance, making sure no one was around it, then began slowly walking downhill toward the river. At times, fog almost enveloped the bridge, lifted for a moment, and then closed in once more.

Inside, the bridge smelled rank, old damp wood and pigeon scat, wet leaves. There were graffiti on the wall, some new, some having been there for the last twenty years, carved by those who seemed to have no other way of announcing to the world that they, too, existed and were of consequence.

The temperature was dropping, and his bad ankle stiffened. He bent over to massage it, working on it until the ache became tolerable. He took a small bottle of aspirin from his coat, shook out two, and choked them down without water.

Below him, Kincaid could hear the sound of Middle River burbling toward the east. He looked through a space where a side board had dropped away and saw the rock on which he stood all those years ago when he looked up at Francesca Johnson. There were flowers along the banks of Middle River in that August, and he had picked a handful of black-eyed Susans for her.

He was glad he had come. It had not been a mistake. Here, in the old bridge, he felt a kind of serenity, and he bathed in the feeling and became quiet within himself. At that moment, he was comforted knowing this place would be his home ground, the place where his ashes would someday drift out over Middle River. He hoped some of his dust would become one with the bridge and the land, and that some might wash far downstream and into larger rivers and then into all the seas he had crossed on crowded troopships or night jets to somewhere.

Rain dripped from the bridge's eaves and through holes in the roof where shingling had long since peeled away. He leaned against a support post and simply let all the feelings, as they had been sixteen years ago and were now, come over him. This, he knew, was a farewell, a letting go and closing down, his way of saying goodbye to Francesca Johnson.

"Goddamnit it all, the turn of things as they turn," he whispered to himself. He said it again, and once more, "...turn of things as they turn." His voice took on the distant thrum of a ship engine north of Cairo, the drone of cicadas in New Guinea jungles, and he recalled some of the words he had written only a year ago for a chapter in Michael Tillman's *Collected Essays on the Road Life*.

*That's all I ever thought about for a long time,
about the going, and early on it never mattered
where. From the beginning, and I see it clearly in
these days, my work in photography was partly a pas-
sion and partly an excuse for traveling. And yet I've
seen a hundred places—more than that, probably—
where I wished I had a separate life for each of them
so I could settle down and live there, so I could get to
know some people well, as others have done, as most
have done. I could have run a general store in that
dusty little hillside town in eastern New Mexico;
joined the ashram in Pondicherry, India; or opened
a garage in a mountain town in southwest Texas or
raised sheep in the Pyrenees or become a fisherman in
some Mexican beach village.*

*The cut is double and hard either way, a matter of
tradeoffs. The road versus the settled life. I'd never
thought much about that until I was in my early
fifties. I met a woman then, and I would have
thrown aside everything for her, the road included.
But there were things in the way of us, and that was
my one chance and afterward I went back out on the
road with my cameras. Now, in my later times, I've
given up the traveling, yet I am still alone. All those
years of breaking camp and moving on (plus my own
reclusive and somewhat antisocial nature, I suppose)
have not equipped me for becoming close to people.*

*So, in that lifetime when you were reading beneath
a yellow evening lamp and wondering about the far
places and maybe wishing to visit them, places where
I've been dozens of times, I was passing by your window and wishing just the opposite. I was wishing for
your chair and your lamp, your family and your*

*friends. It probably was a rainy night when I went by
your house, my gear on the seat beside me, looking for
a place to stay that wouldn't injure my expense
account too badly. I would have found one and slept
and moved on the next morning, remembering your
yellow evening lamp.*

*Still, I made the choice. Yielding to my great flaw
of always pushing on and never looking back, never
feeling an emptiness for that which I had left behind,
except for the woman, I forsook the lamps of home
and chose the road. The consequences are of my own
making, and I have no right to lament what I
brought upon myself.*

Kincaid shook his head and smiled inwardly. I
suppose there's nothing more ridiculous than an
old man's mawkishness, he thought. On the other
hand, he countered, maybe it's just confirmation
I'm still part human.

After a few minutes, he walked out of the bridge.
Enough. He had done what he came to do, to reaf-
firm what his memories told him. To stand in
Francesca's space once more, to see if the feelings
were still as strong as they were then. And they
were. One great love in a single lifetime was
enough for anyone. Francesca had been his great
love, and still was. And he had come to say goodbye. He slapped the side of the old bridge and
began walking with a lighter step than he had
known for some time.

Highway had disappeared, off on some hunting
expedition, Kincaid figured. Kincaid went south
out of the bridge and whistled once, then again,

confident the dog would find him on the way back to his truck. The retriever had been cooped up in the truck for days and needed exercise. Near the top of the hill, Highway caught up with him, panting and happy.

~

"Hell, yes, I know Robert Kincaid," boomed the confident voice of Ed Mullins, photography editor at the *Seattle Times*. "He lives somewhere around Seattle."

"How well do you know him?" queried Carlisle McMillan, shifting the phone to his right hand so he could take notes. A sense of relief washed over him. Finally, someone could transport Robert Kincaid over thirty-six years and could say he was still alive.

"Well, I don't really know him personally, though I've run into him a few times. He's a bloody legend in certain areas of photography, so everybody around here has heard of him except the young snots who went to all the fancy photo schools. None of us know Kincaid well. He's a peculiar guy, nice enough and polite but keeps to himself, does unorthodox work that doesn't sell very well in these times. We've used a few of his photographs in our features section over the years, mostly travel stuff. His work is so refined and subtle that it doesn't reproduce well on newsprint. Plus it's too abstract for general tastes."

"I've seen some of his work, mostly in back issues

of *National Geographic,*" Carlisle offered, hoping the editor would have more to say.

He did. "Yeah, let me tell you, Kincaid was out there, and I mean *out there,* out in the wildest parts of the world, twenty-five years before the rest of us ever got our first Brownie camera. I think it was his shot of a hobo on top of a freight train somewhere in West Texas—tough old tramp with ragged clothes, goggles, scarred hands gripping an iron plate on top of the car—that got me into photography. I could tell by the blurred scenery that Kincaid had been up on the moving train with the 'bo, when he took the photograph. Hell of a shot, one hell of a shot. He got every crease in the man's face sharp, and every scar on the old boy's fingers just jumped out at you. It was in some obscure magazine piece called 'High Desert Rails,' maybe thirty years ago. Still got the article in my files somewhere."

Carlisle wrote, "High Desert Rails" on his legal pad. "Any chance I could get a copy of the article?"

"Sure, if I can find it. Got an address for me?"

Carlisle gave him the address and continued his inquiry. "Have any idea how I might go about locating him? I'm doing some research."

"Hang on a second, let me ask Goat Phillips. He's just coming out of the lab. I think he mentioned he sees Kincaid at a local bar from time to time."

Carlisle heard the clunk of the editor's receiver being laid down on a hard surface. "Hey, Goat... Goat, come over here a minute, got a question for you." Mullins's voice faded as he turned from the phone. Carlisle wondered how the devil Goat, whoever he was, had acquired his name and decided he wasn't all that interested in finding out.

Mumble of indistinct voices, Carlisle picking up a few of the words. "Downtown? Where downtown? What? Route 99 and what?"

The voice came back on, loud and clear. "All right. Goat, here, says he's seen Kincaid at a place called Shorty's, old jazz joint downtown. Just east of where Route 99 bangs across Spring Street. Sax player named Nighthawk Cummings plays there on Tuesday nights, and Goat, being the cool guy he is, goes down there sometimes to hear Cummings and his trio. That's when he sees Kincaid, though he's never talked with him. Feels a little intimidated by him, he says. Goat says Kincaid always sits by himself, drinks beer, and apparently knows this Nighthawk Cummings."

Carlisle scribbled notes: name of the bar, location, saxophone player's name.

"You from the Seattle area or what?" the editor asked. "What's your interest in Kincaid? You say you're doing research? You a photographer or what?"

"No, I'm calling from South Dakota. I'm doing some work in family history and think Robert Kincaid might be a long-lost key to one branch. Listen, I really appreciate the information."

"No sweat, Mr. McMillan. Hope I was of some help."

"Lots of help. Thanks again. May I get your name?"

"Yep. Ed Mullins. Been here forever at this desk,

hardly have time to do any serious field work, myself, anymore. Good luck."

Carlisle hung up and immediately checked the Falls City phone book for the number of a travel agency. He dialed it and asked about routing and fares from Falls City to Seattle.

~

With the temperature balanced on the razor's edge of thirty-two degrees, Francesca Johnson approached Roseman Bridge, her breath turning to thick vapor in the cold. As she entered the bridge, an uneasiness took hold of her, and she stopped, standing and listening hard. She could discern nothing except the sound of pigeons at the far end and water beneath the planks of the bridge floor. She looked down at the flooring and saw muddy footprints, which, by the wetness of them, seemed to have been recently put there.

Drawing her slicker close and hugging herself, Francesca shivered as one might shiver not from cold but from sensing a presence in a darkened room.

"Hello," she tentatively called. "Anyone here?" Her voice reverberated in the hollow space of Roseman Bridge.

"Hello?" she said again, her sense of disquietude building.

At the far end of the bridge, she could see the rain turning to snow, large flakes beginning to fall and lie upon the road. She walked to the south entrance and stood just inside, looking up the hill into the snow. The small grove at the top of the hill was fast disappearing in the swirling, white storm. She had the distinct feeling that somebody, something, was out there, hidden by the trees. A hundred yards up the hill and almost obscured by the snow, a flash of almond darted across the road and into the grove, a farmer's dog perhaps. Above the wind, Francesca was sure she could hear the sound of an engine coming to life somewhere in those trees up the hill.

～

Carlisle McMillan booked himself on a flight from Falls City to Seattle, with an intermediate stop in Denver, for the following Monday. A kitchen remodeling job needed to be finished in Livermore, which would take a couple of days. That would dampen the owner's impatience and bring Carlisle enough money for the plane ticket.

He called the people in Livermore to say he would be there the following morning to finish up their kitchen, adding that the elaborate lazy Susan for the spot in the corner was completed and he would bring it with him when he came. They were pleased and emphasized they were tired of cooking in the garage and eating in the living room. Carlisle was sympathetic and, after hanging up, organized his tools and loaded them in his truck.

~

Francesca started at the blare of an automobile horn. The sound of wind and the concentration of her thoughts on what might be in the trees up the hill ahead of her had covered the approach of Floyd Clark's pickup. He was parked at the opposite end of the bridge, yelling.

"Hey, Frannie. FRANNIE! HARMON SAW YOU ON THE ROAD, AND I THOUGHT YOU MIGHT LIKE A LIFT HOME SINCE IT STARTED RAINING SO HARD. GONNA BE SNOWING LIKE BLAZES IN A MINUTE OR TWO."

She spun and looked through the bridge at Floyd Clark half leaning out his truck window, beckoning to her. Immediately she turned to look south once more, up the hill.

"FRANNIE! LEMME GIVE YOU A LIFT. DIE OF PNEUMONIA WALKING AROUND IN THIS WEATHER." Floyd honked his horn again.

Francesca Johnson stepped out of the bridge and looked up the hill one more time, seeing only white snow in the air and on the road. Floyd was out of the pickup and in the bridge, walking toward her. She turned to look at him, snowflakes already sticking to the roof of Roseman Bridge. Ignoring his words, Francesca began to run up the hill as fast as she could, but with great clumsy effort in her high rubber boots.

Three-quarters of the way up the hill she stumbled and fell into muddy gravel. She managed to stand again, mud and water coating the front of her slicker and dripping onto her boots. Her hood had fallen back and her hair was wet, hanging in shredded twists on her shoulders and clinging to her face. Once more she started up the hill.

Floyd Clark was coming behind her, still shouting. "FRANNIE, HAVE YOU GONE CRAZY?"

Francesca made the hilltop and turned into the trees. Floyd was only a few yards behind her, puffing hard but still shouting about chills and pneumonia. At the far side of the narrow grove, there were tire tracks in the mud, and the smell of exhaust fumes lingered in the protected heavy air of the trees. Francesca Johnson stood there, snow in her hair and coming to lie on her neck, closing from her view a green pickup five-hundred yards down a gravel road and moving away from her.

Floyd took her elbow and guided her back down the hill through Roseman Bridge to where his truck was parked. A small piece of metal lay in the snow at the north entrance to the bridge. She picked up whatever it was and dropped it into the pocket of her slicker.

In Floyd Clark's new Chevy, headed for home, Francesca could only stare at the falling snow and say, "I thought I saw someone I knew. Please, Floyd, don't ask me any more about it. The whole thing was probably just my imagination."

He reached over and patted her arm. "Well, Frannie, we all get strange ideas here and there. Sometimes I think I can hear Marge's voice in the kitchen, calling me down to breakfast."

Back home, Francesca turned on the lights in her

kitchen and pulled the slicker up and over her head. The object she had picked up at the entrance to Roseman Bridge fell from a pocket, bounced once, and lay on the floor near a chair leg. She bent over and retrieved the round piece of metal with an O-ring attached to it. A dog tag, blank on one side. She turned the tag over and let it lie upon her fingers, reaching at the same time for her reading glasses. The words engraved on the tag were difficult to read, and she stepped over to the sink light.

1981
63704
Rabies Vaccination
Monroe Veterinary Clinic
Bellingham, Washington

An address and phone number for the clinic were also printed on the tag. Francesca walked to the kitchen window and looked into darkness, the snow heavy now and whipping at an angle through the yard light. She stood at the window and clutched the dog tag and looked in the direction of Middle River, and she did that for a long time.

12

The Loneliest Highway in America

Robert Kincaid crossed the Missouri River at Omaha, heading west. He barely recalled driving the hundred miles from Roseman Bridge to the big river, fighting snowy roads with his mind full of a woman and an old bridge and all he remembered about them.

He spent the night west of Lincoln, Nebraska, glancing at windows lighted by yellow evening lamps as he drove into town and searched for a motel that would not injure his dwindling cash too badly. It was a long night, snow falling outside, and sleep that failed to come until the late hours. A high-pressure front rode in behind the storm, bringing a bright cold morning the following day. He was up early, pulled on the heavy black turtle-neck sweater, got Harry swept off and warmed, and headed west with Highway on the seat beside him.

Two days later, finally leaving what the storm had left behind, and a little east of Salt Lake City, Robert Kincaid sat at a crossroads for some minutes. He could take a big road northwest toward Seattle, or drop down and travel crumbling Highway 50 one more time. The second route would take him through Reno and then into Northern California. He turned left, heading south to pick up Highway 50, what the signs called the loneliest highway in America. He had done a long photographic essay on the road twenty-five years ago, when it was still a well-traveled highway before the interstates had been constructed.

He mused on what a pilgrimage this was turning out to be as he picked up 50 in the small town of Delta and began the long run toward Nevada and across the high desert. Signs advised keeping the gas tank full because of the great spaces in front of him. He crossed into Nevada around noon, on one of those indecisive days when mountains debate with sky about how things ought to turn out. Sun for a few minutes, then roiling clouds and rain, light splaying through the clouds at times, remnants of snow in the high passes.

Just over the Nevada line was a roadhouse with two ancient gas pumps out front. He filled Harry's tank and went inside to pay. A tall, slim woman with a short, black ponytail and in western dress— boots, jeans, snap-button shirt—took his money and gave him change. Off to his right sat two rows of slot machines. Nobody was shoving money into them at the moment. Four cowboys sat around a poker table, smoking and drinking beer. The smell of hamburger grease hung over everything, and back in the kitchen a cook was banging pans. This place probably hasn't changed in fifty years, he thought, and liked it because of that.

"I've forgotten. How far to Reno?" he asked the woman.

"Three hundred and fifty or so of the longest, saddest, most alone miles you've ever seen. Check your tires, check your oil, check your radiator, then check your intentions. There ain't nothin' livin' out there 'cept snakes and cowboys, and it's hard to tell 'em apart on Saturday nights." She said it loud enough for the cowboys at the poker table to hear.

One of them turned his head toward her and drawled, "Well, Mindy, seems like no one forced you into Hoot's pickup last night. As I recall, you had a Coors Light in each hand and went along with a fair amount of enthusiasm, dancin' as you went out the door."

"Oh, hush up, Waddy," she laughed and got a little red in the face. "You're not supposed to say them things in front of customers."

Robert Kincaid smiled at her, offered a slight wave to the cowboys, and went back to Harry. He pulled out of one of the last best places and headed up toward Sacramento Pass. And out there before him, the silver-green grass. Who had written about that? Someone, eloquently. Maybe in *The Oxbow Incident,* maybe that was where he read it.

The light was good, and he had chased good light for most of his life. With the grass silver-green and old windmills in the distance, there was much to photograph if he chose to do it. But for reasons he didn't quite understand, he lacked the desire to do serious photography, feeling only an unexamined need to keep moving.

And so he moved. Highway 50 worked its way west through country with no signs of life or habitation on either side for long stretches, the desolation causing him to wind on the years, reaching behind and pulling them in. His father had died fifty-one years ago, and that fact alone was enough to make Kincaid feel old. His mother had died in 1937, seven years later.

He remembered his long, secluded boyhood, which foreshadowed the way he would live his entire life. Disinterested in sports or dances, bored and almost antagonistic toward formal education with its unceasing attempts to crush or at least harness his spirit, he became an introverted reader of virtually everything in the Barnesville, Ohio, library. Books, the rivers, the meadows, those were his boyhood friends. Parent-teacher conferences and subsequent efforts to bring him into line and "realize his potential," as one teacher said, were of no use. Still, he seemed to do well enough on the state examinations, and that only increased others' frustration with his behavior, given the apparent lack of attention he paid to his schoolwork.

"If I didn't know better, I'd say that boy got the blood straight down from old Artemas Kincaid," remarked his father one evening after returning from his lifelong job at a valve factory. "Go back a few generations and you'd find Artemas out there on the Mississippi River, earning his living as a banjo player and billiards shark. This boy's got Artemas's restless feet and different ways."

Still, his parents had little to complain about. Robert Kincaid grew up reserved and polite, causing them no heartaches except for the insistent nudging by the local school, and worked summers at whatever job he could find. In high school, the local lumberyard took him on, giving him a job for his last two summers in Barnesville. The Great

Depression bore down just as he graduated, and when his father died only a month after Kincaid had finished high school, he joined the military as a way to support his mother and himself. There, working as photographer's assistant, he discovered what would become his life's work.

As for women, there had been relatively few. Few, but enough. Robert Kincaid was no womanizer, though he easily could have been because of where his work took him and the opportunities that provided. A few brief affairs, a short marriage in midlife, which ended because of his long absences on photographic assignments. And, then, Francesca Johnson. Since Francesca, he had no interest in other women. It was not a studied fidelity nor a painful celibacy he lived for the last sixteen years, not a matter of endurance. After Francesca, he simply was not interested. His time with her had been his defining moment, and nothing of a romantic nature lay outside those boundaries.

So it had been. Early on, trains and freighters, until the big flying boats and DC-3s made it possible to travel the long spaces more rapidly. The 707s after that. Camels and jeeps in the Sahara and Rajasthan deserts. A mule twice, a horse once, though Kincaid had never learned to ride all that well. In Mongolia, there had been no other choice but a horse when he did the 1939 story on the Mongol empires and had been out in the vast, run-on-forever grasslands for nine weeks, tracing the war routes of the Great Khan.

He had received his poundings. Yet aside from the War and a multitude of scrapes and bruises, he had been pretty lucky overall. A few torn muscles, the broken ankle in Maine, a bloodied head in the Congo when a boat had capsized below Stanley Pool. And the near-death experience from yellow fever he picked up from a mosquito in Brazil. A Catholic nun had nursed him through that horrible siege, assuring him in his conscious moments, "Mr. Kincaid, the fourth through the eighth day are the critical ones. You must persevere for eight days and then you will suddenly be well again." And he was, though his skin had retained signs of jaundice for several weeks after.

Robert Kincaid thought of all these things as he drove Highway 50, leaving the region of silver-green grass and crossing the dry emptiness of the Shoshone Mountains.

He said it out loud to the dog. "Damn it, Highway, it's been pretty good when I think back on it—my life, defects and all—and you've been one of the best parts. You know what? We get home, I'm going to call information in Winterset, Iowa, and ask for a Mr. Richard Johnson's number. Just to see what comes back in the way of data. Maybe I should have done it when we were there. No, that would-n't have been right. Anyway, I got all tied up in nos-talgia and didn't think of it. On the other hand, maybe I didn't want to think of it, for some reason."

Highway stood up and licked the side of Robert Kincaid's face. Kincaid put his arm around the dog as they came down out of the Shoshones, with Reno still some distance ahead of them. Both Kincaid and the dog seemed to be smiling as they began looking for a place to lay over on a Sunday night.

13

Shorty's

After changing planes in Denver, Carlisle McMillan rode down into Seattle on a Monday afternoon. Tuesday night was when Nighthawk Cummings played at Shorty's. Carlisle had confirmed that by phone before booking his flight.

"Yeah, Nighthawk's been holding down Tuesday nights for the last five years. Suspect he'll be here as usual on the next one," the bartender had said.

Carlisle checked into a downtown hotel and walked around on one of Seattle's rare sunny days in that season, feeling slightly off-balance by what seemed like a lot of people coming and going. In ten minutes, he saw more lives swirling around him than he would see in ten years out in Salamander, South Dakota. His casual stroll led him to Spring Street, and halfway down the block was Shorty's, just where he had been told it would be.

~

On that same Monday, on the other side of Reno and moving west into California, Robert Kincaid stopped in a town called Soda Springs simply because he liked the name. He gave Harry an oil change and shopped for groceries, loading his bat-

tered cooler with ice, bread and fruit and fresh vegetables, and, of course, Milky Way candy bars. In
mid-afternoon, he wound thirty or more miles past
Clear Lake and two hours later hit the Pacific at
Fort Bragg. The choice of routes had not been
arbitrary. He could have tossed off his decisions as
a desire to stay on less-traveled roads, but it was
clear to him why he had come this way: Fort Bragg,
California, was only ten miles north of Mendocino.

Darkness was twenty minutes ahead and shops
were closing as Robert Kincaid swung off Highway
1 in late afternoon and entered Mendocino. He
parked down the block from the art gallery, left
Highway in the pickup, and walked along the sidewalk until he saw the display of Heather Michaels'
photographs in a front window.

At the door, Kincaid paused, not knowing for
sure exactly what he was doing or what he might
say to the woman he had seen on his last visit to
Mendocino, and was startled to see her materialize
on the other side of the glass. Wynn McMillan's
hand was on the "Open" sign, which dangled from
a string, and was turning it around to "Closed."
Halfway through the process, she halted, still holding the sign with her left hand. She stared through
the glass at the tall, thin man with long gray hair,
taking in the suspenders, the jeans, the black
sweater he wore, the knife at his belt. And she suddenly remembered a short tutorial on the need for
suspenders, which she was given on a beach in Big
Sur nearly forty years earlier.

And as if time itself were swinging back, she
opened the door slowly and stood for a moment,

looking into cool, blue eyes set in a face tanned and furrowed by years in distant suns. The man licked his lips, in the way of getting ready to speak, but couldn't seem to get any words out. He tried again to speak, and failed. He looked at his boots, then at the woman, his face serious and blushing slightly.

"My name is Robert Kincaid," he said, not knowing what else to say.

Wynn McMillan smiled softly. "I think we might know each other, maybe from a long time ago."

~

In the Sea Gull restaurant and bar, Wynn McMillan sat across a table from Robert Kincaid. The beginnings of a northwesterly blew the ocean into whitecaps, and the sound of waves on shore rocks was plain to hear through an open window. Kincaid ordered a beer, Wynn chose white wine. He clasped his hands on the table and stared at them, then raised his eyes to look at Wynn McMillan and smiled, and tried to think of something to say. But he was capable only of letting out a long, slow breath, as if he had been holding it for some time, and allowed a hesitant smile to come onto his face.

"It is you, isn't it? For sure?" Wynn asked, partly in the way of making talk, partly in the way of final confirmation.

"If you're asking about a man who rode a motorcycle into Big Sur in 1945 and made love with a pretty, young cellist on a secluded beach, the answer is yes," he said. "This is kind of awkward for me, probably for you, also."

They sat as old companions more than lovers. Big Sur was a long way back, and they had spent only a few days together in that time.

"You were in Mendocino a week or so ago, correct?" Wynn asked.

"Yes. I looked through the gallery window and saw you. I might not have recognized you except for the way you moved your hands and maybe the way you fix your hair as you did then, how you touch the comb in it from time to time."

Robert Kincaid looked straight at Wynn McMillan, and it struck him that thirteen years of difference in their ages seemed much greater now than it did in 1945. At sixty-eight, he bore the rime of age and knew it. But she was fifty-five and held onto some remnants of her youth.

"Do you still play the cello?" he asked.

"Yes, with friends, mostly. Sometimes we give small concerts here. And you? Photography, wasn't it?"

"Yes, I've pretty much been on the road all these years. A lot of the work has been overseas." He drained the last of his beer just as a waiter came by to ask if they were all right. Wynn's glass was still three-quarters full. Kincaid ordered a second beer. He pulled out a pack of Camels, noticed there was no ashtray on the table, and slipped the smokes back into his pocket.

"I wrote you two or three times, after leaving Big Sur," he said, when the waiter had gone.

"I left there not long after you did." She said

only that, and that was enough in the way of explanation about letters never received.

The next part was going to be more difficult, and Wynn McMillan wondered for a moment whether it was necessary to mention Carlisle. She decided this man before her, whose last name she had not recalled until he introduced himself twenty minutes past, had a right to know. That, plus Carlisle's search for him.

"Did you marry, have a family?" she queried as a way of moving into the subject.

"Married a nice woman in 1953. We were divorced a few years later, no children. My work didn't lend itself to marriage very well, me being gone so much. And you?"

It was there, the time for telling. Wynn McMillan fretted with her wineglass and, for a moment, looked out the window at unsettled water, the Pacific becoming more turbulent as the northwesterly was reinforced by incoming tide. Two men and a woman sitting together at the bar broke into strident laughter at something the bartender had said. Kincaid glanced at various sea relics decorating the restaurant's walls, then focused again on Wynn McMillan as she began to speak.

"I was married to a man for six years in my late thirties and early forties," she was saying. "The dream of becoming a symphony cellist had faded, maybe because I never became quite good enough, technically, maybe because of the bias against women certain artistic directors had in those days. Anyway, I turned too quickly toward something else and lurched into a marriage that was a foolish idea at the start and got a lot more that way as time went on. I've been happy, though. I've met several nice men here on the north coast." She was circumventing what she knew had to be said and was aware of it.

The waiter returned with Kincaid's beer and left.

"No children?" Kincaid inquired, straightening one of his suspenders, adjusting his belt, touching the knife fastened to it.

Wynn McMillan remembered those movements from their days in Big Sur, Robert Kincaid checking to make certain his accouterments were all in place, making sure he was prepared for whatever came his way. She adjusted the napkin on her lap, took off her glasses and laid them on the table. After looking at him for a long moment, she reached out and took one of his hands in hers.

"We...we have a son, Robert Kincaid...you and I have a son. His name is Carlisle."

~

On Tuesday morning, Carlisle McMillan stopped by the *Seattle Times* and introduced himself to Ed Mullins, the photo editor with whom he had spoken by phone.

"Hey, Mr. McMillan. Glad you stopped by. Didn't know you intended on coming out to Seattle. I found Kincaid's 'High Desert Rails' piece only last night. Had it filed under 'trains,' for some stupid reason. Should've put it under 'Kincaid.'" That would've made more sense. Let's go over to the Xerox, and I'll run you off a copy."

The man seemed extremely busy, his phone constantly ringing and people drifting by his desk to ask questions or offer suggestions about projects. After the article had been copied, Carlisle thanked the editor again and left. At his hotel he drank a beer with his lunch, reading the article while he ate, and took a long nap afterward. He was only killing time, his sense of anticipation coming up on a breaking point. Nighthawk Cummings would take the stage at nine. When Carlisle awoke, he still had six hours to wait. He decided to go to Shorty's around eight, just in case Robert L. Kincaid arrived early.

Meanwhile, he rehearsed what he would say, none of it sounding right. All of it sounding nosy, prying, if not insulting. From what he had learned in his conversation with the editor and a brief meeting with Goat Phillips, who left the photo lab for a few minutes to speak with Carlisle, Kincaid kept to himself and didn't seem all that approachable. In fact, they viewed him as somewhat eccentric.

Carlisle worked on what he might say to Kincaid, and the more he worked, the dumber it got. In fact, it got downright laughable.

"Hi, I'm Carlisle McMillan, and I have reason to believe I might be your bastard son."

Or: "Hi, I hear you once owned an Ariel Four motorcycle. Hell of a machine."

Or: "Hello, there. Did you ever make love with a woman in Big Sur, California?"

Maybe: "Ever hear of a female cellist named Wynn McMillan?"

With that level of subtlety, Kincaid understandably might just get up and walk, if not run, out the door, ending the whole business forever.

Finally, Carlisle decided it was going to be a lot like carpentry. Take a look at the job when he got to Shorty's and start figuring it out from that point. At seven o'clock, with city lights outside his window, he put on a clean pair of khaki slacks, a flannel shirt, and pulled on his leather jacket.

The elevator took him to the lobby.

The street took him to Shorty's.

The doorman said there was a three-dollar cover charge.

The doorman added, "There's only one two-spot table in the whole place, over by the wall there, and Nighthawk has us reserve that for a friend of his who comes almost every Tuesday night. Since there's only one of you, we'll appreciate it if you sit at the bar."

Carlisle said he understood, took a seat at the bar and ordered a beer, looking hard at the table near the wall with a "Reserved" sign perched on the blue checkered tablecloth. On the small stage not far from the reserved table, a drummer was setting up his kit.

~

Robert Kincaid and Wynn McMillan talked a good part of Monday night. Halfway through the conversation, he suddenly remembered, with guilt and self-censure, Highway back in the truck. They walked with Highway along the headland in a stiff wind, clouds skittering across a quarter moon. She told him about Carlisle's growing years, and back in the restaurant where they had a late dinner, she described how their son had become a master carpenter under the hand of a man named Cody Marx.

And she told him about Carlisle's search for a man named Robert Kincaid, how he had come by that name through his research coupled with what she, Wynn, had remembered. Kincaid listened, trying to make the adjustments in his mind, the reorientation to how his life suddenly seemed to lie before and behind him. What had been his private truths up to this point, the great sense of being alone in the universe and all the rest, were jumbled by what Wynn McMillan had spent four hours telling him.

Around eleven, she said, "Robert, I think we should telephone Carlisle and tell him you're here."

Kincaid agreed and walked with her to a pay phone at the rear of the bar. The place was half-full at that hour and alive with animated conversation. Wynn dialed Carlisle's number in South Dakota and finally replaced the receiver after the tenth ring.

"Heaven knows where he might be," she said and smiled. "He's a little like his father, always moving around. If it's okay with you, I'm a bit tired of the bar atmosphere, and maybe we could go to my house and continue our talk."

Late, sometime after one in the morning, he asked if she would play the cello for him, the piece she had played in Big Sur. Wynn sat on a straight-backed chair and played Schubert. Robert Kincaid sat in a bentwood rocker, listening, his head bowed, hands clasped on his lap.

When she finished, he thanked her and said, "Wynn, I have always remembered how warm the sand was in that September of 1945. That's one of the things I have always remembered."

Wynn canted her head and smiled gently at him. "I know, Robert Kincaid. I remember that, too."

Kincaid had a small piece of work coming up, photographing a minor story for a Seattle month-ly. It would pay three hundred dollars, and he needed the money. Wynn and he agreed, however, that one way or another, the three of them—Wynn, Kincaid, and Carlisle—should meet and spend time together.

"I'm not sure we qualify as a family," she said. "But it just seems right that all of us sit down and hear the stories of our lives from each other, what we did and didn't do, recount the failures, remember the triumphs."

He volunteered to drive her to South Dakota, if necessary. But, because of her job, Wynn said she would ask Carlisle to come home for a visit and that he likely would arrive on the first plane out after she told him what had happened.

Though Wynn offered Kincaid her couch for the night, he politely declined, but said he would like to meet her for an early breakfast if that was all right. He felt a need to be alone, to think his thoughts, and to put into perspective everything Wynn had told him.

The following morning, Tuesday, the two of them stood by his truck for some moments, as he prepared to leave for Seattle. In the daylight, while a rested Kincaid put his arm through the truck window and petted Highway, she could see distinct traces of the rider from Big Sur. He limped a little now, but the broad shoulders and slim body were still intact. The same intensity was there, too. And the eyes she always had remembered, eyes looking through and beyond to whatever it was he saw, something only he could see and had no way to articulate except through his camera lenses.

She smiled at him. He reached out his hand to shake hers and then stepped forward and put his arms around her, smelling her hair as he had smelled it on a beach in Big Sur, thirty-six years ago. She laid her head against his chest and pointed toward the ocean. "The whales still come by in March," she whispered.

~

Nighthawk Cummings walked onto the stage at two minutes past nine to scattered applause from a three-quarter house, began snapping his fingers and counting off. He brought up the old Selmer tenor saxophone and came in with the pickup notes on the second beat of the next measure. The quartet was off and running on "This Is a Lovely Way to Spend an Evening," Nighthawk's tenor smooth and creamy with the potential for an edgy, hard-bop sound lurking just beneath the cream.

The table with the reserved sign on it was still empty. Carlisle McMillan tried to concentrate on the music, but couldn't. He looked at the table, then the door, repeating the process every minute or so.

Raised the child of Wynn McMillan, cellist, Carlisle's ear was reasonably sophisticated, but not in this genre. Though Nighthawk Cummings announced the tunes, he spoke softly and indistinctly into the microphone, as if everyone there already knew the names of the songs and his mentioning of them was ceremonial rather than necessary. Carlisle caught something about "Green Dolphin Street" and another one called "Oleo" apparently written by someone with the last name of Rollins and a first name he couldn't quite make out when Nighthawk said it.

After the first set, and the lone two-spot still empty, still reserved, Nighthawk Cummings came over to the bar and ordered a Glenlivet. He stood three feet away from Carlisle and leaned against the bar, sipping on his drink, surveying the crowd. People stopped by, old fans by the way they walked up and shook his hand, talking knowledgeably about the music.

"Yeah," Nighthawk said to one of them, in a slow, drawly fashion. "Joey hit an augmented-seventh chord just in front of the tonic—he doesn't usually do that on 'Stars Fell on Alabama'— and I heard a sound in my head I hadn't associated with that tune before."

Another one requested "Autumn Leaves," and Nighthawk responded, "We're going to get to that one, maybe next set. Got a friend who always likes to hear the song, and I'm waitin' to see if he shows up tonight."

Alone again, Nighthawk glanced over at Carlisle and said, "Evenin'. Don't think I've seen you in the club before."

"I came here for a specific reason," Carlisle smiled.

Nighthawk Cummings narrowed his eyes. "And what would that be?"

"I'm looking for a man named Robert Kincaid."

Nighthawk's face was impassive. "And why would you be looking for a man by that name?"

Carlisle went through his family-tree explanation, hoping Nighthawk might volunteer information. Cummings took another sip of Glenlivet and said nothing.

After waiting a decent interval, Carlisle went on. "I understand he comes in here and that you and he might be friends."

"If we were, I'd have nothing to say. I never talk about my friends unless they want me to. That's a good way to lose good friends. Nice to meet you, man. Gotta get ready for the next set."

Nighthawk Cummings walked off toward the stage, picked up his tenor saxophone, and loosened up, his dark fingers running the golden keys, unbelievably fast scales in E-flat major while the other three musicians took their places.

~

By eight o'clock on Tuesday night, Robert Kincaid had returned home, fed Highway, and bedded him down. He sat in his kitchen and ran through what Wynn McMillan had told him. All of it had a dreamlike quality to it. A strange life had become a lot more strange in the last twenty-four hours. He walked to the filing cabinet and removed a box of photographs. For some time he sat there, looking at Francesca Johnson. A few days earlier, he had stood in her space and remembered. And, god, how he still loved her, even allowing to himself that things like that remembered are better than they ever were.

In some way, Francesca should know about Wynn and Carlisle. He wasn't sure why that was required, it just seemed right to him at the moment, something to do with full truth and honesty. Three years earlier, he had left a letter with an attorney. The letter contained instructions that, if something happened to him, the attorney should send the letter and other items to an address in Madison County, Iowa. He decided he would redraft the letter and drop it by the attorney's office when chance provided.

Staring at Francesca's image, he began to weep, and the weeping turned to confused, choking sobs. Kincaid bent over his kitchen table and let the tears run as hard and fast and long as they needed to. And he spoke to himself between the sobs. "Jesus…Jes…all this time…all this, all this…all this damn, long lonely time…I was not alone."

Highway came over to sit beside him, nudging Kincaid's arm.

Robert Kincaid now had to confront the deep sense of guilt he felt. The guilt about fathering a son and not being there to help Wynn McMillan during Carlisle's growing years. Wynn had tried her best to allay the guilt, saying she never had been sorry about bringing Carlisle into the world and that there was no way Kincaid could have known.

Her words helped a little, but Kincaid knew he would carry his guilt through the rest of his life. Circumstances were one thing, the fact that he had not been there was something else, and there was no way of reaching an accord with that. Maybe there was some way he could make it up to her and Carlisle.

Thirty minutes later, he looked at his watch. Nine o'clock. The weather was good outside, and Nighthawk would be just getting underway. Dammit, a man who's just come close again to Francesca Johnson and who's also discovered he has a son he never knew ought to do something to celebrate or at least mark the occasion. A great love lost, a son found. One did not trade off for the other, the things were too dissimilar, but a balance he never felt before had come into his life. He could catch the ten o'clock ferry.

Kincaid walked over to where Highway was stretched out on an old blanket. He squatted down and stroked the dog. "I'll be back in a little while, my friend. I'm going to pay a visit to our buddy, Nighthawk." He put on his coat and gently closed the door behind him.

~

Carlisle pulled up the sleeve of his leather jacket and looked at his watch. His eyes were watering from the cigarette smoke permeating Shorty's, and he blinked twice, trying to see the watch. Ten-thirty, and the two-spot by the wall was still empty. He shifted positions, ordering his third beer of the evening.

Nighthawk Cummings and his group were into it and really cooking, running through Ellington's "It Don't Mean a Thing." Nighthawk had stepped back and was letting the piano player take an extended solo while the bass player hunched over his instrument, moving spiderlike hands along the fingerboard of the stand-up acoustic. The drummer was bobbing his head, putting in accents just where they ought to be. Carlisle noticed Nighthawk grin and raise his hand in a subtle greeting toward the door of Shorty's.

Carlisle swiveled on his stool and saw a man with long gray hair come through the entrance. His palms started to sweat as he watched the man work his way through the tables and take a seat at the two-spot by the wall. From the photographs he'd seen in *National Geographic,* he was absolutely sure it was Robert Kincaid. A waiter came by the table, delivered a beer to Kincaid without having taken an order from him, and picked up the "Reserved" sign. Nighthawk brought up his tenor and traded fours with the piano player as they started to wind down the tune.

After two more songs, Nighthawk spoke into the

microphone. "Going to play one for a good friend of mine. Tune I wrote a while back, called 'Francesca.'" Nighthawk counted off a slow tempo and then blew a throaty, melodic figure in the first measure, the melody pronouncing the woman's name. The man at the two-spot brushed his hair back with both hands. He leaned forward and wrapped his fingers about his bottle of beer, staring at the bottle, listening.

On the second chorus, Nighthawk lowered his horn and began to sing in a gravelly baritone,

> *Francesca, I do remember you*
> *and the old ways of summer.*
> *You wore silver*
> *when the long days were yellow...*

At the end of the song, the piano player segued the group out of B-flat major into E minor and gave Nighthawk an introduction for "Autumn Leaves." By the wall, the gray-haired man continued to stare at his beer bottle. As Carlisle watched the man, he understood what Wynn had meant when she remembered his eyes, old eyes, older than those of a single lifetime. He tried to imagine, and had no difficulty doing it, the man at the table as a silhouette riding a big road bike along the Santa Lucia terranes. He could see him crossing the high bridges and leaning into the curves while a young woman held onto the rider's waist and let her long hair blow back and tangle with the wind of their passing.

When Nighthawk closed "Autumn Leaves" with

a plangent run of semitones, he looked down at Robert Kincaid sitting there by himself, a long way from anywhere, a place Nighthawk Cummings understood. Kincaid looked up at Nighthawk, smiled, and nodded his appreciation for the songs.

"Thank you very much. Be back in a few minutes," Nighthawk said over the microphone and placed his tenor on its stand. He stepped from the stage and walked to the two-spot, sitting down and shaking hands with Kincaid. As they talked, Nighthawk shifted his eyes twice toward where Carlisle McMillan sat at the bar. After a minute or two, the gray-haired man looked at Carlisle.

Maybe I handled this stupidly, Carlisle thought. It was clear to him these guys, particularly these guys, Nighthawk and Robert Kincaid, if that's who he was, lived in an entirely separate universe from most people and especially from his own generation. Not as forward, not the coming-at-you-baby attitude the sixties and seventies had engendered and which seemed to be escalating in favor.

Robert Kincaid turned once more and stared at Carlisle. He said something to Nighthawk, and the saxophone player got up and walked to the far end of the bar. Nighthawk ordered a shot of Glenlivet and began a conversation with the bartender. Kincaid looked for a few moments at his beer, recalling the snapshot Wynn McMillan had brought to breakfast with her. A phone behind the bar began ringing as Kincaid stood and with a slight limp walked toward Carlisle, smiling the warm and embracing smile of a father who has not seen his son for a long time.

14

All the Strange Hours

Carlisle stayed in Seattle for two more days, and the hours were strange ones, he and Robert Kincaid talking on and on. They sat in Kincaid's small cabin, at the kitchen table, talking more as new-made friends than as son and father. If that latter bond were ever to be forged, it would take longer than a handshake and a few hours of conversation. But each looked long and hard at the other, trying to bring into focus what apparently was true yet seemed unreal. Carlisle McMillan, the misbegotten son of a lone rider who now sat across a kitchen table from him. Robert Kincaid, the rider of far places and distant dreams, now wrestling with the idea of a son whose face he could see and whose voice he could hear.

Kincaid, struggling with the words, said over and over again how sorry he was for not being there to help Wynn see Carlisle through his growing years. "I wrote her, Carlisle, I really did. We simply lost track of each other."

"Yeah, I was pretty angry and confused about it when I was young." Carlisle talked and studied the small cabin. The ceiling needed work, showing stains where a roof leak had dripped through. "Wynn has been a fine mother, unconventional in her ways and lifestyle, but really tough in her own fashion. She never once has said anything unkind about you, accepted her fifty percent of the whole business."

He went on to talk about Cody Marx, his teacher in life and carpentry. Kincaid listened closely. "Well, I'm sure grateful to this Cody Marx. Is he still alive?"

"No, he died a while back. It was pretty hard for me to take, his dying. Without Cody I'm not sure where I might have ended up."

He hesitated for a moment, then asked, "Did you love Wynn back in those days? Or is that a dumb question?"

Kincaid fiddled with a pack of Camels, took one out, lit it with a match. The match book carried a brief message: *Sea View Motel—The Place to Stay in Astoria, Oregon.* He smoked the cigarette, wiped the palm of his left hand across his chin.

"No, I'd be telling less than the truth if I said I did, Carlisle. We weren't together very long. Those were unstable years for a lot of us, trying to get our lives and heads organized after the War. There was something more between us than just fooling around on a beach, I think we both sensed that, but it never had a chance to take flight. Our intentions were decent, Wynn and I agreed on that the other night. But we were young and, well, it's kind of hard to explain and...." He shook his head, looked down at his hands on the table.

"Wynn told me as much over the years," Carlisle said, talking directly to Robert Kincaid. "Look, I finally got rid of my anger. Made a tentative peace with it all." For a moment, he was tempted to finish the sentence with "Dad," but he couldn't bring himself to use that word. His connection with the man before him was one of blood and maybe a little more after their time together, but not yet at the place where "Dad" seemed right to him. It might not ever get to that place.

Kincaid began dabbing at his eyes with a yellow bandana he pulled from the right hip pocket of his faded jeans. He looked up at Carlisle. "Damn, lot of years wasted, Carlisle, when we could have been doing things together…lot of years."

He flapped the bandana. "Sorry, lately I seem to be wiping my eyes quite a bit."

Carlisle McMillan felt a wetness in his own eyes and reached across the table, clasping Robert Kincaid's shoulder. In spite of Kincaid's age and thin frame, the shoulder still carried a fair amount of muscle. The silver medallion around Kincaid's neck had slipped from inside his shirt and swung in the lamplight. Something was written on the medallion, but the word was indistinct beneath scratches and tarnish. Some day Carlisle wanted to ask about the medallion, but put it off for the moment.

"Look," Carlisle said, still grasping Kincaid's shoulder. "I figure it's a lucky man who knows his father's face. Far as I can tell, I got lucky."

He asked if he might see some of Kincaid's photography. Robert Kincaid brightened at the suggestion and began pulling sheets of transparencies from the file drawers. If words came hard for him, the images were a way of showing the son before him how his life had been lived. He brought out a small, portable light board and set it up on the kitchen table. They spent an entire afternoon the following day looking at Kincaid's work, Robert Kincaid talking on and on about the road years, about what shot was taken when and where, about the smells and light each photograph brought back to him. Carlisle recognized several of the photographs from the *National Geographic* articles he had copied.

Portions of Kincaid's work surprised him. While most of it had a rather grand poetic vision underlying it, some was hard-edged, high-contrast work in black and white. He was particularly fascinated with what Kincaid said had been shot as part of a UNICEF project called "The Slums of Jakarta."

"That shoot was a son of a bitch," Kincaid said, clenching his jaw as he studied the prints arrayed on the table. "Did it for expenses only, because it was worth doing. It's good to get involved in that kind of work occasionally. Helps get rid of the airbrush quality people seem to have in thinking about underdeveloped parts of the world. It's not all orangutans and elephants out there, not all colorful ceremonies and candy-striped sunsets with flamingos flying over Africa.

"Here," he opened another box of prints. "This set came from a private piece of work I did last year at an old folks home downtown. Did a portrait of each one of them and gave them each a print, matted, framed, ready to hang or set on their bureau or give to their families if they had any, and most of them didn't. That was real satisfying. They got themselves all excited and dressed up for the sessions. Some of them were bedridden, so I had to get creative and not make it look like a hospital."

Robert Kincaid was smiling with pleasure as he sorted the prints, holding them up one at a time for Carlisle to see. "This fellow had been a railroad engineer for a short-haul line in the western part of the state, had two strokes, partially paralyzed. This woman had been a cabaret singer. Garbage collector, truck mechanic, former illustrator of children's books, prostitute. There are a million good stories in that home, just waiting for someone to write them down." He returned the prints to the box and smiled again.

While they cooked a simple meal that evening, Kincaid turned to his son. "I have a favor to ask of you, Carlisle."

Carlisle waited, saying nothing, but noting how serious Kincaid was as he spoke the words.

"When I die, I'd like it very much if you'd burn all the negatives, slides, and prints. I'll make sure everything is in this filing cabinet in the kitchen and the one in the bedroom."

Carlisle started to protest, but Kincaid held up one hand, indicating he had more to say. "This has to do with a view of life and death that's almost impossible to explain in words. It's more of a gut-level feeling that time and I are old partners, that I'm just another rider on the big arrow. My life is worth no more than what I have done with it, and I've always seen the search for immortality as not only futile but ludicrous, just as elaborate coffins are a pathetic attempt to evade the carbon cycle."

Kincaid stirred a pot of vegetable soup, looking

over at Carlisle, talking as he moved the ladle.

"That and the fact of having my photographs floating around out there where I can't exercise judgment about how and where they might be used. The dock worker in Mombasa or the young woman in a Mexican field might end up in cheap travel brochures. The one of the men putting out to sea in the six-oar boat might find its way into an advertisement for rowing machines. Almost as bad, they might end up in some exhibition with people evaluating my work while nibbling on Brie and crackers, searching for deep inner meaning in photographs that never had any deep inner meaning to start with. They're just pictures, after all."

"I could make sure none of that would happen," Carlisle said.

"Yes, and I'd trust you to do that as long as you lived. But then what?" Kincaid took two cans of beer from the refrigerator and handed one to Carlisle. "Besides, it goes beyond how the images might be used. It goes back to what I said before. When I die, I'd like the floor swept clean behind me, all traces gone, nothing left. It's just my way, Carlisle, just the way I see things."

"All right. I'll do what you say, I promise that, even though I wish you felt otherwise."

Kincaid thanked him while looking at the floor, scuffing his boot across it. Suddenly he gasped and bent over slightly, pain coming to his chest, the dizziness and feeling of nausea sweeping over him again. He leaned against the refrigerator, sweat pebbling his face.

"My God, what's wrong?" Carlisle exclaimed

and went over to him.

Kincaid waved him back. "I'll be all right in a minute or two, just some stupid thing having to do with being old," he gasped. His sun-browned face had grown noticeably gray under the tan, and he struggled to catch his breath.

Carlisle helped him to a chair. After a few minutes, Kincaid managed a thin smile and said, "It's okay. Have these damned attacks once in a while. They go away, and I feel fine."

"Want me to take you to a doctor?" Carlisle offered, concerned.

Highway came over to the table and put his chin on Kincaid's leg.

"No. I've been to one." Kincaid reached down to run his hand over the dog's neck, wrapping his fingers in the thick fur. "Doctor says I'm okay, just some fool thing having to do with an irregular heartbeat or something. It passes. I'm learning to live with it."

Carlisle didn't believe him, but let it go at that. Robert Kincaid obviously had his own view of himself and his life, a view Carlisle still didn't grasp completely and maybe never would.

An hour later they were laughing together and shaking their heads, when Carlisle discovered his father had been in Salamander only a week before. Carlisle asked if Kincaid might like to visit him in South Dakota and see his work, that he could help with plane fare if need be. Kincaid said he would like very much to do that, maybe come spring when the weather would be better and he and the old man above Lester's could get around a little easier, get over to Leroy's to hear Gabe play tangos. Carlisle said he would drive out to Seattle sometime, bring his tools with him, and fix up the cabin a bit.

They talked of photography and the work of carpenters, about learning to do things right. Robert Kincaid told the story of how he once spent twenty-four hours watching a single leaf on a maple tree in autumn. From dawn to sundown and on through the night as the moon moved across it, he studied the leaf, metered it, framed it. He equated it to playing scales or maybe even etudes in music, learning about how light alone could change an object.

Carlisle understood and related how Cody Marx would make him do the most routine tasks over and over until he had them down cold. He laughed, "Preparing the surface, those words that strike fear and boredom into the hearts of amateurs, was something Cody never let me forget. I spent most of my first year's work with him doing nothing but sanding, using a hand plane, and stripping old paint."

The following day Kincaid drove Carlisle to the Seattle-Tacoma airport, Kincaid's camera gear stacked between them on the seat. When the boarding call for Carlisle's flight came over the public address system, both of them stood and looked at each other.

"Take care of yourself," Carlisle said earnestly, meaning it in the most literal sense.

Robert Kincaid grinned. "I'm carrying a lot of miles, Carlisle, but most of the time I feel like I have quite a few more left in me." He looked at his watch. "Well, I better go make some pictures, earn a little money."

Carlisle started to follow the crowd heading toward the gantry. He turned, shouldered his way back to where Robert Kincaid was standing. Kincaid looked at him, straightened an orange suspender, touched his belt, and remembered airport security regulations had advised leaving his knife in the truck.

"I'll be looking for you in the spring," Carlisle half blurted out the words, having trouble with a catch in his throat. An agent at the desk was issuing the final boarding call for the Denver flight.

"I'd like you to see my work," Carlisle went on, his voice sounding hoarse. He cleared his throat and spoke softly. "I suppose…suppose a son always wants his father's approval."

They stepped toward each other. Carlisle put down his bag and swung both arms around Robert Kincaid. Kincaid hugged his son, in turn.

"Ah, dammit, old man, dammit it all, anyway. You hang in there, hear me?" He pulled back one of the orange suspenders and gently let it slap against Kincaid's back.

At the entrance to the gantry, he turned and looked at his father one more time, his face serious, thinking of a lone rider traveling the roads of Big Sur all those years ago, when the world was simpler and freedom had been all that mattered to a certain breed of people. Robert Kincaid stood as straight as his sixty-eight years would allow, shoved his hands in the pockets of his faded Levi's, and nodded at

Carlisle, then smiled in the warm and embracing way of a father saying goodbye to a son he had not seen for a long time and with whom he had not spent enough hours.

From behind him, along the concourse, he heard the boarding call for a Singapore flight, and out on the tarmac a 747 lined up and began to roll, heading for Jakarta or maybe Bangkok or Calcutta. The agent closed the gantry door behind Carlisle McMillan, and Kincaid shifted his eyes, watching the Boeing sweep upward and disappear in the overcast, content with the thought of a big plane heading for somewhere and that he was no longer alone.

15

All Traces Gone

For a while, the bright new world of Robert Kincaid cut through the damp fog of Puget Sound. He cleaned his cabin, pressed his clothes, and spent long hours telling Nighthawk what had happened, talking enthusiastically about visiting Carlisle in South Dakota, sometime in the spring. He exchanged letters with Carlisle and Wynn, each of them noting events and memories they had neglected in their conversations. He even made an appointment for a complete physical examination.

But things turn as they turn. Three weeks after seeing Carlisle off to Denver, and four days before his examination, Robert Kincaid died of a massive heart attack, alone in his cabin, where he was found by a neighbor alerted by Highway's barking. He had left the phone numbers of Wynn and Carlisle with his friend, Nighthawk Cummings. Nighthawk called Carlisle, who then telephoned his mother with the news of Kincaid's passing. Wynn McMillan had wept softly and asked about funeral arrangements. Carlisle said Kincaid's remains had already been cremated and would be scattered at an undisclosed location by the law firm that handled his affairs.

As promised, Carlisle returned to Seattle. A note in Kincaid's handwriting was attached to the kitchen filing cabinet: "Carlisle, everything is in this cabinet and the one in the bedroom. Use the trash barrel out back. Thanks. It has taken me a while to get used to the idea of you being my son, but I'm getting there. And, from what I can tell, you're all a father could ask for. If anything happens to me, Nighthawk will take care of Highway."

Carlisle sat at the old kitchen table for an hour, the refrigerator's hum laid over what few memories he carried of Robert Kincaid, wishing there were more. He gathered up newspapers and started a fire in the trash barrel. As he looked again through the files, Carlisle momentarily considered reneging on his promise to Robert Kincaid. But that was not possible; his word had been given. More than that, he had come to a tentative understanding of what Kincaid meant about the finality of it all. And he recalled his father's words: "...the floor swept clean behind me, all traces gone, nothing left."

On that clear, sharp day in December, Carlisle stood before the trash barrel. One after the other, he dropped slides and negatives into the fire, watching the life work of Robert Kincaid turn into ashes and smoke. The grinning dock worker in Mombasa, the girl in a Mexican field. The tiger coming out of long grass near Lake Periyar in India, the hard-faced man looking down from a combine in North Dakota. The distant peaks of the Basque country and men putting out to sea in the Strait of Malacca. All of them curled and died in a trash barrel on a December morning in America.

It took Carlisle three hours to carry out his task. He often would stop and hold a slide up to the light, looking at it one more time before dropping it into the barrel. At the end, there was left only a manila envelope and a white box in the bottom drawer of the bedroom cabinet. Carlisle opened the envelope and peered inside. It was full of letters, twenty or so. He took one out and noticed it had been sealed but never posted. The rest were the same and all addressed to a Francesca Johnson, RR 2, Winterset, Iowa.

Carlisle remembered the article on covered bridges his father had done in the sixties. And the name "Winterset" belled in his memory. He recalled the town had been mentioned in the article. And wasn't there a song named "Francesca" Nighthawk Cummins had played? Carlisle fished a matchbook from his pocket and copied the name and address on it. Temptation began to grow within him, and he fingered one of the letters, turning it over in his hands. No, that wouldn't be right, not right at all. He thought for a few more seconds and dropped the manila envelope in the barrel.

Carlisle watched the envelope catch fire and then opened the white box, carefully removing a sheet of paper laid over a thin stack of black-and-white prints. The top one was of a woman leaning against a fence post in a meadow somewhere. She was, Carlisle thought, extraordinarily beautiful in the way that only a mature woman can be, standing there in tight jeans and with her breasts clearly outlined against her T-shirt. Her black hair was blowing slightly in morning wind, and she seemed almost ready to step out of the picture toward him.

Immediately below that print was another of the

same woman, but less graphic, the woman cowled and the photo almost impressionistic. In this case, she was pensive, as if she were about to lose something she could never find again.

Carlisle held aside those two photographs and dropped the others into the barrel. The flames leaped as they caught the paper. He stared again at the two remaining prints of the woman.

Pulling a deep, long breath, Carlisle McMillan looked out across Puget Sound. In the distance, he could see a blue heron looping across morning water. And on that day, at the same moment a woman in Iowa set out on her walk to a place called Roseman Bridge, he let the photographs of Francesca Johnson slide from his hand and into the fire.

~

Final Notes

So we end a book of endings. As I recounted in *The Bridges of Madison County,* Francesca Johnson died in January of 1989. Her ashes were scattered at Roseman Bridge, at the same place Robert Kincaid's had been scattered eight years before. In 1981, after helping Carolyn with the birth of her second child, she returned home and called the veterinary clinic in Bellingham, Washington. She was informed that Robert Kincaid had switched to another clinic some months before. Using a phone book in the Des Moines public library, she obtained the names and numbers of every other clinic in the Seattle area. One of them, indeed, had a current address but no phone number for a Robert Kincaid. Mr. Kincaid, she was told, had a golden retriever.

As Francesca was making preparations to travel to Seattle, a UPS truck delivered a box. In the box was a letter from a Seattle attorney, which began, "We represent the estate of one Robert L. Kincaid, who recently passed away."

Also in the box were Kincaid's cameras, a silver bracelet, and a letter he wrote to Francesca in 1978, which he never subsequently revised to include Carlisle McMillan. Thus, in the end, Robert Kincaid did not quite sweep clean the floor, leaving a few of his things in the care of Francesca Johnson, for whatever reasons were his alone.

As for Carlisle McMillan, his own story concerning what is known as the Yerkes County War and a woman who changed him from a boy to a man is worth the telling. Maybe I'll get to it one of these days.

Nighthawk Cummings is nearing eighty-five and lives in an apartment in Tacoma. A vertebra problem, which causes his arm to numb, ended his playing days, but he still gets out the horn once in a while, usually at dusk, and ruminates on "Autumn Leaves" and thinks of his good friend, Robert Kincaid. Though Nighthawk knows the story of Robert Kincaid and a woman named Francesca, Kincaid never mentioned her last name or where she was from. Hanging on the wall of Nighthawk's apartment is a photograph of a covered bridge, signed by Robert Kincaid. For reasons not clear, Nighthawk is drawn to the photograph and usually looks at it while he plays.

Highway, the golden retriever, was adopted by Nighthawk's nephew and lived another four years after Kincaid died. And Harry, the '54 Chevy pickup? That was one of the last pieces I had to uncover. Through all my research, Harry seemed as much alive as Francesca, Highway, Robert Kincaid, and everyone else. Finally, I located him. He has been affectionately restored and now lives in South Dakota. Carlisle McMillan was kind enough to let me drive Harry up and down a country road near a place called Wolf Butte. Looking through the windshield, bouncing along, I imagined without effort all the miles, all the grand, questing miles he and Robert Kincaid traveled together and what they saw, chasing good light. Carlisle also suggested I open the glove box. Tucked behind the cracked lining of that compartment is a wrinkled business card. On the card are printed these words: Robert Kincaid, Writer-Photographer. Oh, one more small piece of information: In the glove box, wrapped in a rag, is a single roll of Kodachrome II 25-speed film, unused.

I leave you with this, a moment from my life, my wanderings:

> *Creek from somewhere in the coastal mountains.*
> *coming fast here*
> *over volcanic sand,*
> *giving the water*
> *   a blue-running-to-lavender color.*
> *Farther down the beach,*
> *an hour earlier,*
> *I had seen a bull elephant seal,*
> *thousands of pounds of him.*
>
> *So it was the California coast,*
> *in autumn when the sand was warm.*
> *Knee-high rubber boots*
> *gave me purchase*
> *and the freedom to wade.*
> *I stood in the creek,*
> *followed it with my eyes*
> *to where the Pacific began.*
>
> *The mother of Carlisle McMillan*
> *once lay on this beach*
> *with a man named*

Robert Kincaid,
another shooter who followed
the light
because the light
was on the road.

That was 1945.
He had survived
the War
and rode a motorcycle
through here afterward.
High on the rim of their lives
they laughed
and drank red wine
by the water.
And from that
came a boy-child, Carlisle.

Blue creek,
and I adjusted the tripod,
did it again, leveled the Nikon,
thinking about Kincaid,
about Wynn McMillan,
water around my boots,
first wind of morning
in the cypress.

The curator of a museum
where the photograph eventually hung
called and asked
if it truly
was water over blue sand.
Didn't look like

water over blue sand
she said.
I told her
a volcano
had done it,
centuries ago.

   I just came by
   later on...

      ...I and Robert Kincaid.

And isn't it a long way home. Long way.

End